Berta Bulkeley Jones, Harriettee Blakeley, Canon Marmon

An account of the minister of Freiburg in Baden

Partly adapted from the German

Berta Bulkeley Jones, Harriettee Blakeley, Canon Marmon

An account of the minister of Freiburg in Baden
Partly adapted from the German

ISBN/EAN: 9783741191718

Manufactured in Europe, USA, Canada, Australia, Japa

Cover: Foto ©Andreas Hilbeck / pixelio.de

Manufactured and distributed by brebook publishing software
(www.brebook.com)

Berta Bulkeley Jones, Harriettee Blakeley, Canon Marmon

An account of the minister of Freiburg in Baden

THE MINSTER OF FREIBURG.

An Account

of

THE MINSTER OF FREIBURG

IN BADEN.

Partly adapted from the German

of the late

VERY REV. CANON MARMON

by

BERTA BULKELEY-JONES

and

HARRIETTE BLAKELEY.

FREIBURG in BADEN, 1886.
B. HERDER.

"— and he is blest whose outward eye
The graceful forms of Art may trace,
While his free spirit, soaring high,
Discerns the Glorious from the Base,
Till, out of dust, his magic raise
A home for prayer and love, and full harmonious
praise.
Where far away, and high above,
In maze on maze, the tranced sight
Strays, mindful of that heavenly love
Which knows no end in depth or height,
While the strong breath of Music seems
To waft us ever on, soaring in blissful dreams."

John Keble.

Dedication.

THE following little volume is the result of
the melancholy condition in which two lone Pilgrims to Freiburg found themselves in the year
of Grace 1884, when, fired with enthusiasm at
the sight of the Minster it was in vain for them
to hope to enter into its glories, since neither
of them understood a word of the German tongue or, could decipher a letter of its blinding
type, so could profit by no "Guides" either two-
legged or in Duodecimo.

Had it not been for the kindness of an
English resident of Freiburg, Colonel Roberts,
who took pity on their benighted condition,
they might have left the place with but a slender knowledge of the deep teachings and wonderful interest of this, perhaps the most beautiful,
Minster in Europe.

TO COLONEL ROBERTS

then is this little sketch *dedicated , in gratitude*
for his great courtesy, with the hope that this
book may prove an addition to the pleasure of

many English-speaking visitors to Freiburg, or
a sufficient inducement to many Lovers of Faith
and Beauty to halt a while in the delightful old
Capital of the Mining country of the Black Forest.

Many thanks are likewise due to Frederick Jameson Esq. Architect, for his very kind assistance
in all the architectural portions of this work.

We must acknowledge also with most sincere
gratitude the kindness of the late very Rev. Canon
Domcapitular Joseph Marmon († 11 Nov. 1885)
in allowing the free use and translation of much
of his valuable little German work on

Unserer Lieben Frauen Münster.

H. B. and B. B. J.
Easter 1885.

Index.

Notice.

1. Strangers wishing to inspect the Minster may address themselves to the Sacristan. — Should he not be present, apply at No. 29, Minster Platz N. E. corner, where he resides.

2. During Divine Service, walking about and all disturbance, are most strictly forbidden.

3. The Sacristan has strict orders to politely reprove, or if absolutely necessary, to send out of the Minster any persons behaving irreverently at any time, in the Sacred building, those who are talking or laughing loudly, smoking, keeping on their hat (if men), having eatables, bringing in dogs, soiling or cutting the seats, the floor &c. &c.

A Table of the Divine Service throughout the year. Sundays and Festivals.

Sundays and Festivals.

Summer (Spring to Michaelmass)		Winter (Michaelmass to Spring)	
First Mass	5 o'clock	First Mass	6 o'clock
Missa vot. B. V. M.	7 „	Frauenamt	7 „
Military Mass	8 „	Military Mass	8 „
Mass	8.30 „	Mass	8.30 „
Sermon	9 „	Sermon	9 „
High Mass	9.45 „	High Mass	9.45 „
Low Mass	11 „	Low Mass	11 „

At 2. p. m. Sermon.

2.30 Vespers — Gregorian Music.

On the 1. Sunday in every month Devotions for the Confraternity of Corpus-Christi at 4. p. m. with Sermon at 2. p. m.

In the evening the Devotions of the „Salve Regina."

Week Days.

(Spring to Michaelmass)		(Michaelmass to Spring)	
First Mass	5 A. M.	First Mass	6 A. M.
Our Lady's Mass	7 „	The same	7 „
Mass (not every day)	8 „	Every day	8 „
Missa Cantata	9 „	The same	8 „
Low Mass	10 „	The same	10 „

Every evening, with the exception of the last three days of the Holy Week, Devotions of the „Salve Regina."

A Table of all the Feasts observed throughout the year.

With hours of Divine Service.

Feast of the Immaculate Conception in Advent. Dec. 8.

Christmas - Festival of the Birth of Christ. One of the four chief Festivals. Early Mass 5.30 Dec. 25.

Feast of the Proto-Martyr St. Stephen. Dec. 26.

On New Year's Eve Sermon. 5. p. m. with short Devotions and Exposition of the Blessed Sacrament. Dec. 31.

On the last Sunday of the year, Thanksgiving. Missa Cantata at 6 and 7 a. m.

New Year's Day. Festival of the Circumcision. Jan. 1.

Feast of the Epiphany (Consecration of Holy Water and Salt). Jan. 6.

Feast of the Purification, or Candlemass with Procession and Benediction of Tapers. Feb. 2.

Ash Wednesday, 1. day of the Lenten Fast. Sermon. at 9 a. m. Benediction of Ashes, after the Sermon.

Once a week during Lent until Palm Sunday, an evening Sermon.

Feast of St. Joseph. Mar. 19.

Feast of the Annunciation, or Lady-Day. Mar. 25.

On Palm Sunday, no Sermon. Blessing of the

Palms, and Procession. In the Mass, the Gospel of the Passion is sung as well as that for Palm Sunday.

Maundy Thursday, 6.30 Mass, 8 a. m. Sermon. High Mass with solemn Consecration of the Oils, by the Archbishop. Procession and Deposition of the Holy Sacrament. Ceremony of the Stripping of the Altar. Washing of the Feet.

Good Friday. Sermon at 9 a. m. The Ceremonies of the Day.

On Wednesday, Thursday and Friday in Holy Week at 5 p. m. Tenebrae.

Holy Saturday the Ceremonies commence at 8 a. m.

Blessing of the Fire or Light in the Porch. Solemn Benediction of the Paschal Tapers and of Baptismal Water.

Mass of the Resurrection, with solemn Bell ringing at the Gloria (which is silenced from Maunday Thursday in token of Mourning). In the Evening at 6 p. m. Devotions of the Resurrection with Procession.

Festival of the Resurrection. Easter Day. One of the Four great Feasts of the year.

Easter Monday, also a Festival of Obligation.

On Low, or White, Sunday (Dominica in Albis) At 8 a. m. Mass for the First Communion of Children. High Mass, 10. a. m. In the afternoon, at 4 p. m. Devotions of the Blessed Sacrament.

Feast of St. Mark. Procession to Loretto at 6 a. m. April 25.

On the first three days of Rogation week, Beating the Bounds at 6 a. m.

In the month of May Devotions every evening at 7.30.

Festival of the Ascension.

Whitsun Eve. 8.30 a. m. Solemn Benediction of Water for Baptism.

Whitsun Day. Festival of the Gift of the Holy Ghost. — One of the Four principal Festivals of the year.

Whitsun Monday. Festival of Obligation. Annual Confirmations.

Festival of Corpus Christi. Solemn Procession of the Blessed Sacrament through the town. Lady Mass at 5.30 a. m. High Mass 7 a. m.

During the Octave Solemn Vespers. On the Octave, Procession in the Minster before the 8 o'clock Mass.

Perpetual Adoration before the Blessed Sacrament from 4.30 p. m. of June 30th to 9 o'clock a. m. of July 2.

Festival of the Assumption of the B. V. M. One of the Four High Festivals of this Arch-Diocese, and also the Dedication Festival of the Minster. August 15th.

The Nativity of the B. V. M. September 8th.

Feast of the Patrons of the Town S. S. Lambert and Alexander. Procession. The Procession takes place only on Sunday immediately following the feast of the Patrons of the Town, round the Minster after the Sermon. Sept. 17.

General Benediction of the Minster. Sept. 17.

Festival of All Saints. No Sermon in the afternoon. Vesper at 1.30 p. m. Visitation of the Cemeteries November 1.

Festival of All Souls. Sermon at 9 a. m. After Sermon, Requiem for all the Departed. In the afternoon Visitation of the Graves.

Nota Bene. The Music at High Mass at 9.45 every Sunday, apart from the great solemnity and reverence with which it is performed, is a very great musical treat. The most magnificent Masses, Ancient and Modern, are beautifully sung, accompanied by a full band, as well as the grand organ.

During Advent no instruments are used, the effect of the unaccompanied voices being of singular and touching beauty, especially in the opening "Kyrie eleison, Christe eleison". The performance of Gregorian music at Vespers is also excellent.

General Survey of the Cathedral.

THE Cathedral, dedicated to "Our Beloved Lady", is a stately monument of the Catholic Faith, erected by the willing sacrifices and offerings of our forefathers, and is the great ornament and pride of the town, holding the dearest place in the heart of every true Freiburgher.

The traveller sees from afar the heaven-pointing spire, which tells him he is approaching the "Pearl of the Upper Rhine" — the friendly Zähringer town, whose streets are made musical by crystal streamlets fresh from their mountain cradles, whose buildings are full of remembrances of old feudal days.

The Minster was built at two different periods and in two very dissimilar styles, — the Gothic and the Romanesque, but the former prevails so much throughout the whole building that at first sight the whole appears to be of about the same date, and the Romanesque portion (the transepts) presents no violent contrast to the rest, because it belongs to the transition period of that style. And the Gothic spires of the weathercock towers and the long line of the choir

in front of them prevent the point of union
from being observed.

In Gothic architecture every line points hea-
venward. The pointed arch — the soaring
steeple — the lofty tower — all cry "Sursum
Corda"; and in this lies the deep religious spell
of Gothic architecture, that every line rising
from earth meets a kindred line, and together
they soar towards heaven, while in the round
arch the lines rising from earth bend over, and
fall to earth again.

All the beautiful capabilities of Gothic art
have been developed in this building with a lavish
wealth and an endless variety in every part
that fills the eye and mind with amazement.

So little plain wall is visible that it seems
only built for the purpose of holding the lace
work of the windows together.

Those windows of the nave which are next
the transept are left in the pure Romanesque
style (round bars and balls), while the opposite
windows are of the early Gothic with its simple
bar and measure.

All the remaining windows are architectu-
rally richer than these; but those on the north
side are all narrower than those on the south,
and the north side is throughout less richly decorated than the south. The walls are strengthened by buttresses to bear the pressure from

within, and the same service is rendered to the
middle walls of the nave by flying buttresses,
beautifully sculptured as if with lace edgings. —
These are faced with little towers which not only
give great strength, but also add greatly to
their beauty and that of the whole building, as
do also the gables, finials and figures of many
saints, heroes and animals, with which the
whole is enriched.

Wide galleries within and without make
every part of the roof easily accessible. Gutters
collect all the rain-water and lead it through
the mouths of grotesquely fanciful gurgoyles
to fall far beyond the foundations of the Minster,
in many a cascade, from head of lion, dolphin,
fabled beast, or humorous figure, to the frequent
terror of the unwary pedestrian in the market
place below.

The steeply pitched roofs not only harmonize
well with the architecture, but are of manifest
practical use in heavy falls of rain and snow. The
leaning roof of the side-aisles is brought up to
the centre of the clerestory windows and at this
point is a second gallery.

In former days the roof was of itself a great
ornament to the town; for it was composed of
old glazed tiles in patterns of green, red, blue and
yellow, similar to those that cover now the old
Kaufhaus below. — How lamentable that this

1 *

grand and artistic handiwork has been allowed
to decay, and that dark slates replace the beautiful
decorations of our forefathers!

The east end is completed by the twelve-sided
choir, having a flat roof of stone surrounded by
a gallery of lacework in stone carving. But
the great glory of the Minster is the spire of
filagree stone work, which, in richness, boldness,
and nobleness of form and flight, far surpasses
every other spire in Europe, excepting perhaps
the Sister Cathedral of Strasburg, built, it is
supposed, by the same architect.

The basement story of the tower, whence
rises this spire, is hollowed out into a magnificent arch which forms the porch of the Cathedral, so that, standing in the market place you
see at once the spire — the tower — and the
rich sculptures of the porch beneath.

Above this porch, where the roof commences,
a richly sculptured gallery surrounds the tower,
and at that point the four-sided tower becomes
an octagon, giving thus a far richer architectural surface to the middle portion of the tower
than to the story below.

From a second gallery starts, at the east
side, a splendid open staircase in rich stone work
by which the bells are reached; and, again ascending, the flat stone roof of the bell chamber
is found to form a terrace from whence soars

aloft the hollow pyramid of stone fret work of
the spire, forming an octagon, on the square.
tower.

Nothing can exceed the beauty of this as
seen at sunrise rising above the mist, like a
pyx of some ancient goldsmith's filagree work —
glittering in the golden rays, or at sunset when
the warm red colour of the stone causes it to seem
enveloped in a violet mist against the opal sky.

The Minster stands from west to east and
is not quite opposite the rising sun at midsum-
mer. This position as we know symbolizes our
faith in Christ the Sun of Righteousness, Who
appeared in the east, and in anticipation of
Whose second coming the dead are buried with
their faces to the east, and the living turn to
the east in Prayer and Creed.

The Cathedral was a creation of the middle,
or so called, dark ages. Now, dear reader —
look at it either near, or from the Schlossberg-
heights above — let your eye glance from that
fleur-de-lis of stone at the point of the spire
where at eventide the stars seem to rest and
commence with the carved angels that ornament
it on every side, down to the pinnacled roofs and
lacework galleries crowded with the Saints and
Heroes of the Church, and say if those ages can
truly be called 'dark' that were capable of
imagining and of producing works of such splendour

and which adorned Europe with hundreds of similar creations of architecture and sculpture. Of course, the middle ages have their dark points, as has every other age in the world's history, but we cannot deny that compared with its colossal works in architecture and sculpture, its poetry and its faith perpetuated in stone and metal — the works of this age are indeed puerile and devoid of true beauty for the most part.

The large open space round the Minster was formerly the town cemetery, and on it stood a chapel with three altars. Before its door was a huge crucifix which now is removed to the centre of the old cemetery, and close to it was a Gothic tourelle where the guild of bakers maintained a perpetual light. This lamp was typical of the eternity of the soul, the life after death, and served as a reminder to those still living, to pray for those gone on before. These held all their place till 1740 — 44 when they were removed to a large field beyond the town walls, — now no more the burial place for Freiburg — and the chapel, dedicated to St. Michael, was there re-erected by the Cathedral Trust-fund, but it had already been closed for burials in 1513, in consequence of several outbreaks of the Plague or Black Death.

The Statues outside the Minster.

ON THE TOWER. The Minster is spoken of
in the archives as "Our beloved Lady's Building", being dedicated to the Blessed Virgin.
In harmony with this title is the group above
the point of the great arched entrance to the
open porch: namely, the Coronation of the Virgin, a group once richly coloured and gilt, now
worn to its original stone colour. The Virgin
and her Son sit facing each other on a throne
of Romanesque design, the Virgin's hands are
meekly folded on her breast as she bends before
her Son, Who with one hand offers her a sceptre
and with the other points to two angels who
hold a crown above her head — other angels
bear candelabra and swing censers, while two
female martyrs with book and palm complete
the group. On the same level are seated four
figures, protected by canopies, clothed in official
habit, and partly robed in long mantles fastened
by a fibula in the form of an eagle, to which
the figures point in a marked manner, two with
the left, and two with the right hand, which
gesture may denote firstly an appeal to their
own consciences, as to their righteous admini-
stration of justice, and secondly, an assertion of

their imperial commission by this badge of office. On the pedestals appears the same imperial eagle on a shield. The figures have long hair rolled over the ears, two are bareheaded and two wear birettas.

It has been suggested that these represented the Duke of Zähringen and his followers, Counts of Freiburg, but as at the date of the erection of this tower no such persons as those latter existed, the far more rational explanation is, that these figures typify the Four Cardinal Virtues: Justice, Temperance, Prudence and Fortitude — according to a passage from the celebrated Rationale div. off. by William Durandus, Bishop of Mende A. D. 1270, who says: "The four walls of the Church symbolize the Four Cardinal Virtues." The first figure on the right hand undoubtedly represents Justice, having the right foot laid over the left leg and a sword level across his knees as we read in the old archives of the town of Soest "a judge shall sit on the judgment seat as a furious lion, putting his right foot over his left knee".

On the brackets supporting these figures are carved groups and animals signifying the errors and crimes which bring people under the arm of the Law, and their opposite virtues.

Thus beneath the stool of Justice we see a hare playing with a lion's mane, showing the defence of the Weak and the subduing of the Strong, by just laws well enforced. Beneath the feet of Prudence we see a bull, an ass, a ram, and a hare, denoting certain forms of Heresy and Obstinacy, which Prudence will extirpate.

Fortitude tramples a dog beneath his feet, emblem of Profligacy, and evil living, while on the bracket supporting Temperance is a most curious and elaborate "double entendre". An ass is represented who has flung off his burden and is enjoying himself among some thistles — a symbol of disobedience, idleness, and self-indulgence. But then again if you look at the other possible interpretation, the ass, who has the command of an overturned sack of oats, and might have enjoyed a surfeit of good things, becomes a model of Temperance by dining off the homely thistle of his own accord.

In olden times the Freiburg Courts of Justice were always held (as were also other meetings of great public import) in the open porch of the Minster, which are well typified by the solemn air and uniform position of the presiding figures, who hold the lowest place as representing the first foundations of the civilized life. —

Next above stand Kings and Queens, the Nursing Fathers and Mothers of the Church. The Emperor Rudolf of Hapsburg, during whose life the tower was finally completed, and who died

1**

A. D. 1291, is here with his Empress Anna
von Hohenberg-Heigerloch, on whose finger is a
regal ring, and whose tomb is in Basle Cathedral.
Rudolf is denoted by the Ciborium which he
carries reverently, as though hardly venturing
to touch it. This has reference to a well known
incident which occurred at Meggen near Lucerne.

Riding in the country one day he overtook
a poor priest who was conveying the Blessed
Sacrament to a dying parishioner, by rough ways
and swollen streams: "Shall I", cried the Emperor,
"ride at ease, while the Lord my God is carried
afoot?" and thereon dismounting he placed the
priest in his saddle, and he himself led the horse
the whole way. Rudolf, who was born 1" May,
1218, in the castle of Limburg on the Kaiserstuhl,
was the son of Heilwig von Kyburg, and through
her was connected with the house of the Zähringer.
The election of Rudolf to the Imperial throne
was hailed with enthusiasm by all Germany, which
had long been torn by dissensions; but the
Counts of Freiburg considered him especially
their own and always sided with him in all disputes.
These reasons perfectly explain the presence of
this royal pair on the tower of the Minster.

At the same level, to the north and south,
stand two knights armed, but bare-headed, with
mantles flung round them — probably representing the shield-bearers of the royal pair.

Above these again stands a Bishop, probably meant for Conrad of Constance, and a female Saint, generally supposed to be St. Ursula, who shields beneath her spreading robe a number of kneeling persons, though some maintain that this figure represents the Advocacy of the Blessed Virgin for Freiburg.

At this level the statues north and south are again Imperial, wearing large crowns and ermine. That to the south bearing the Orb is doubtless Charlemagne, who restored peace to his country after long disorganization and was crowned Emperor by Leo the 3ᵈ in Rome Dec. 25, 800 A. D. The northern figure is Louis the Pious, his son, whose long monkish robe recalls the fact that his own rebellious children compelled him to enter a cloister and leave the kingdom in their hands. The Orb was the symbol of dominion in the hands of Roman Emperors, surmounted by an image of Victory. From the days of Constantine, the Orb is surrounded by a circle and crowned by a cross. The Emperor Henry II. was solemnly presented with this Orb by Pope Benedict VIII. at Rome, in the year 1014. With this Imperial ball, sign of earthly dominion, God the Father and God the Son are frequently represented.

St. Katharine and St. Michael and the Dragon are at the south east corner of the tower, and facing them an Abbot — probably St. Ber-

nard — and a Deacon. The highest portion is
surrounded by the 12 prophets — David with
crown and harp being among them, and on the
pinnacles round the tower are the angels of the
Resurrection blowing trumpets. Wonderful is it
that, in all these centuries, neither storm nor
time have visibly injured these figures, exposed
to every blast, to earthquakes and to sieges,
and wonderful indeed must be the work which
has been able to withstand such trials and,
apparently, may stand as much again.

Statues on the South side.

Coming round the south side of the Minster
we first perceive on the top of the buttress near
the rose window a small figure of David playing
on the harp — above him is another king,
name unknown. In the double niches of the
buttress that stand next in order, are seven figures
of the apostles and John the Baptist, all full
of individuality — finally four unknown kings
of a Byzantine type, supposed to be the oldest
figures in the Cathedral, the last of which
bears a reliquary suspended by a cord round
his neck. On the pedestals of these figures are
ram's and bull's heads, and under the last king
stands a man holding a sun-dial. At a much
later period another and larger sun-dial was

placed on the south face of the transept, about which can still be read the entry in the account book of the trust fund, dated "A. D. 1512. Item: 6 pounds 5 shillings to the mathematician who made the sun-dial above the Door of Benediction".

These buttresses are finished at the top as shrines, each containing the figure of a Saint, a Martyr, or a Bishop.

In the gable of the beautiful side door which is formed by columns and pointed arches, is the Agnus Dei looking at the standard of the cross which is supported by its foot. Before it is a chalice. This is one of the most ancient symbols of Christ, very common even in the catacombs of Rome, adopting an idea prominent in Holy Writ, as where Isaiah cries "Send ye the Lamb to the ruler of the land" Is. 16. ch. Also the exclamation of St. John Bapt. : "Behold the Lamb of God." And in old Romance the young Titurel aptly sings (Strophe 680): "A Lamb that carried a blood red standard in his hoof, by this sign has helped us to victory and overcome the power of Lucifer."

The old Byzantine round arched doorway of the transept, supported by numerous small columns is now alas! obscured and partly covered by the great loggia of the Renaissance Period, which at one time formed part of the lectorium, or screen, between the nave and the choir.

This though in itself a beautiful work of art has by a singular want of correct feeling and fitness, been allowed to remain in the Minster, shocking the eye both within and without by its utter incongruity with all its Gothic surroundings. But it is so great a protection and convenience that its ultimate removal is very hopeless.

In the gable of the old door sits St. Nicholas, on a "Sella Curulis", evidently Byzantine. This is called the Door of Benediction, because, from its proximity to the font, all persons coming to be baptized, or churched, enter that way.

A third door leads into the choir, and above it are carved the Death and Coronation of the B. V. Mary, showing her death bed surrounded by the apostles, Peter holding a Holy water vessel. Above is seen God the Father in whose hands is the soul of Mary as an Infant newly born into heaven, while sympathizing angels gaze on the scene — the apex is filled with the Coronation of Mary by Christ, two angels play the harp and organ.

On the sides of the arch are Mary with the Infant Christ, and St. Christopher with his burden of Deity, and above is St. George, formerly Patron of the town, and a few other figures of very old but excellent workmanship.

Sculptures on the North side.

THE door leading into the choir on the
north side is surrounded by very ancient and
perfect figures depicting the history of man. The
point of the arch is filled by a strange representation of the ambition of Lucifer, who endeavours
to plant his throne (which he carries in his.
hand!) beside the throne of God. See Isaiah
14. ch. 13. v.: "I will exalt my throne above the
stars of God. I will be like the most High."
God the Father by a motion of the hand stays
his advance.

In the circle of the arch is first seen — the
Creation, the formation of the firmament, stars,
and orbs — then the Earth with plants and trees,
animals and man. Adam formed from the earth.
God breathes into him a soul. Eve taken from
Adam's side, their union by God as man and wife.
— The hallowing of the seventh day.

On the two sides of the arch we see the
Fall, the Expulsion, and the Sentence of Labour.
Adam digs the soil, Eve spins, and the child
fetches water.

The arch of the entrance door of the north
transept is filled in by a fresco, well renovated
in 1868 by Sebastian Luz, which represents
the Virgin enthroned with the Infant Jesus. On

one side is St. John the Evangelist, on the other a
Bishop, probably St. Lambert or St. Conrad, Patrons
of the Church, and beneath kneel the Donor
and Donatrix of this embellishment, with their
coat of arms — a white escutcheon with a red
banner on it, indicating the de Montfort family.

The entrance to the north aisle is quite
unornamented, and this side of the Minster
does not possess the beautifully decorated buttresses, niches, and gurgoyles of the south side.
The most notable perhaps, though certainly a
comparatively recent addition since the Great
Schism of 300 years ago, is a very prominent
figure of an old nun pointing to a single tooth.
The reformer of the day it appears, had thrown
open all the convent doors of Freiburg, and
declared that every nun that had a tooth left
in her head, should be given a husband. And
this old person is supposed on the strength of
her one tooth to be clamouring for her privileges.

The gurgoyles of a Cathedral in old times
filled somewhat the place of the Punch and
Charivari of modern life — and the jokes, abuses,
or absurdities, of the day were often gibbetted
on high among the gutters and water spouts in
imperishable stone. Two or three remarkably
preserved figures of greyhounds appear to be
springing from the roof to the street below.
A St. Michael, three apostles — and a prophet

complete the line of sculptures to the north —
and on a pillar near the rose window to the
west, we recognize King Solomon.

The Great Porch.

BEFORE entering through the iron gates of
the porch, let us examine the inscriptions and
figures deeply graven on the stone walls, for they
are as old as the Minster itself and control the
weights and measures of the town to this day.
On the north west wall is cut in outline the
standard size for the household loaf, its length
height and ˋthickness. Also for the "Penny
Roll" with the dates 1270—1317—1320, which
were years of famine and of plenty, worthy of
note. Next is the Standard ell — an iron bar
let into the stone —, by which all woven stuffs
are sold. Then comes the square outline of the
Measure of charcoal, stamped with a fleur-de-
lis and close to it the inscription "A. D. 1295.
The measure eight times filled shall be a load of
wood". Opposite these on the south wall are
engraved the legal sizes for bricks and for tiles,
also the fathom, marked by two iron pins. Next
is incised in 15ᵗʰ century Gothic type, clear as
if cut yesterday, the dates and rules for the two
annual fairs, as follows: "A fair shall be held
on the next Monday and Tuesday following the

Feast of St. Nicholas, and another on the next Tuesday and Wednesday following the Feast of All Saints. A day will be allowed both before and after the fair for preparation and clearing."

On the north side we must now notice a coat of arms twice engraved, undoubtedly belonging to the date of the erection, probably the arms of one of the founders.

A kind of railing of spiral lines crosses them both from right to left, the meaning of which is forgotten.

The magnificent arch which frames the porch is supported by a huge cluster of twin pillars, from whose beautifully sculptured capitals springs the pointed arch above the apex of which is the three-sided niche containing the Coronation of the Virgin already described on page 7.

The great iron gates, closed after sundown, are the work of a blacksmith named Fr. Ign. Mägle, in 1820.

————

Twenty-eight slender pillars of marble, with beautifully carved capitals, stand round the inside of the porch to a height of about 25 feet from the ground, these still bear many traces of formerly bright gold and colouring. From the pavement rises a double row of deep seats along both walls. Here in old times the courts sat, disputes were decided, councils held, public charities dispensed, and penitents made public atonement. The porch is now much frequented for the mid-day rest and meal of neighbouring work-men and their little children, who meet them from the school, while the good housewife opens her humble store and spreads it on the bench. From the uppermost of these steps rise on each side 14 pillars, joined by pointed arches and on each pillar stands a figure, under whose feet the capital of the pillar forms a niche or canopy, with carvings of leaves, flowers and groups of figures of great interest. The allegorical figures thus supported tell the whole *Story of the Christian Life*, its helps, its hindrances and its outcome — in the Redemption of Man and his elevation to glory. The Crucifixion, the Judgment and Paradise, forming the culminating points, fill the pointed gable of the great west door way.

1. At the north east corner, standing near the great door way, and facing all who come into the porch, we see our Lord, clothed in a long white seamless robe (typifying the Unity of the Church), Who beckons with His raised finger calling all men into His Kingdom — the Church. His other hand holds the written Word.

2. Now, turning back to the north west corner of this line, we are shown how the Prince of this world strives to allure and hinder those

who would obey the gracious inner voice, by promises of worldly gain and pleasure.

3. But nearer still to each entering soul, the very first figure on each side of the porch is a Guardian Angel, on whose girdle is inscribed "Nolite exire", "Come not out". Follow not the seductive voice of the world but pass within. Next the Guardian Angel of the porch stand "the fleshly lusts that war against the soul".

4. First "The World" offers with outstretched hand the cup of pleasure; in her other hand is a pair of gloves (in early times these were looked on as a type of Vanity and Luxury). On her head is a crown, and all the front portion of her body is gorgeously robed, but her back is bare, and all over it crawl loathsome reptiles and vermin, scorpions, toads, serpents, &c. On the base is inscribed "Calumny". — This figure shows the bitterness that follows satiety — the remorse too surely brought by the world's seductions, the bad results of sinful lives.

It is a line of expression that runs throughout the Gospels that "the World" signifies what is opposed to and estranged from God, and those whose highest aim is the attainment of honours and wealth, of flattery and luxury, of sensual and fleshly indulgence — while to the kingdom of God belong those who follow Christ in self-abnegation and self-control, using all their powers and gifts for the advancement of His Kingdom and for the glory of God.

5. Beneath the next figure is written "Voluptas" showing what the World has to offer, represented by a woman scarcely clothed by a goatskin, type of impurity, and holding out a goblet of wine. — But next to her stands another

6. Angel for the protection of man, whose girdle bears this inscription : "Watch and Pray, that ye enter not into temptation". Matt. 26. ch. 41. v. Without Prayer and Vigilance it is impossible to escape the seductions of the World and the Flesh.

Beyond the Guardian Angel, who will assist Man in his resistance to the Prince of this world, are eight figures, typifying the way to Christ on which our good Angel would lead us.

As to the names of these figures — they are not placed in historical order, but they very evidently denote Man's call to righteousness, and the position of each figure so agrees with the natural course of the consecrated life, that we have no hesitation in naming them as follows :

7. Aaron, the first ordained and chosen *Priest*, holds the foremost place on the path of righteousness and the return of man to God — He holds in his hand the book of God's Law and the censer of offering and atonement.

8. *Praise* is the natural sequence of the reunion between God and Man, and David with his harp is its fitting emblem. The next figure may be considered as either Sarah, or Elizabeth the wife of Zachariah — both types of strong

9. *Faith,* under very similar circumstances. But the fact of this figure being next to Zachariah, and that, next to him, stands St. John the Baptist, makes it almost certain that this represents the Family who stand at the Threshold of Christianity — and Elizabeth's evident attitude of stepping forward, denotes her meeting the B. Virgin at the Visitation, when her exclamation "the Mother of my Lord" was a second very salient act of *Faith.*

10. In natural sequence follows St. John the Preacher of *Repentance,* robed in camel's hair and holding the usual banner, type of Christ the Lamb of God, for Whom John was to prepare the way by the conversion of hearts.

11. Very appropriately then is he succeeded by Abraham, true type of humble *Obedience,* whose willing offering of his son foreshadowed that of which John was the precursor. A mysterious hand issues from a cloud and seizes the point of Abraham's raised sword or knife, at which Abraham gazes astonished. The result of *Faith* and *Obedience* will certainly be *Forgiveness ;*

12. and of this the fittest emblem is Mary Magdalene who stands next holding the box, of precious ointment the gift of LOVE.

And now Man, delivered from the paths of Sin, absolved and trained to Praise, to Believe, to Repent, to Obey, and as a natural consequence to be Forgiven and to Love, draws near to the marriage chamber of the Lamb; and here we see 13. 14. 15. 16. 17. the Five Wise Virgins standing with lamps and trimmed burning, typifying the whole Free Will and Powers of Humanity brought into subjection to the Will of Christ, and permitted to stand next to Christ, the Heavenly Bridegroom, for Whose second coming the Church looks and waits.

Figures ressembling these are found on Basle, Strasburg, and probably other Cathedrals, the idea of thus depicting the Christian life often recurs in the mystic and poetic plastic teaching of the middle ages.

We now start afresh with the figure of the beckoning Saviour with which we began, Who stands calling every soul of man to enter the Church, the marriage chamber. — This Union of every soul with Christ in His Church is typified 18, by the fair woman in bridal attire of white and gold, who stands next to the Heart of Christ — Her head is crowned, the standard of the cross, sign of victory, is in her left hand

and her right offers the chalice of the B. Sacrament to all who follow her banner. She looks toward the figure of the Synagogue, which faces her on the opposite wall.

This figure together with the following eight which stand inside the arch of the great west doorway, is on a larger scale than the rest, and they represent persons more nearly connected with the actual work of Redemption. Next the allegorical Church stand the Firstfruits of the New Dispensation — the Three Kings of the East.

19. The first bends his left knee and on his right supports his crown, he raises the chalice of myrrh on high, while the Angel leans from heaven and holds the star before their eyes according to the ancient belief that the Star of the Nativity was carried by Angels in front of the travelling Magi or Kings.

Tradition and art have at all times agreed to represent these Wise men of the East as Kings or Princes, according to the prophecies of Isaiah and David.

"The Kings of Tharsish and of the Isles shall bring presents, the Kings of Arabia and Saba shall bring gifts — surely the Isles shall wait for thee and the ships of Tharsish first to bring Thy sons from far, their gold with them, unto the Lord thy God."

The number of the gifts — three — points to the threefold gifts given only by Royalty to Royalty. One king is always represented as a negro, for "Saba" or "Arabia". From the very earliest days of the Church in the Catacombs, these kings were thus represented, and their names Gaspard, Melchior and Baltazar were names of very ancient use.

And now leaving unnoticed for a moment the wonderfully complicated groups and scenes from early Church history that fill the niches beneath these statues and also the central sculptures of the door way, let us cross to the right side of the porch where is told the story of the reunion of God and Man in the Incarnation.

20. First stands the angel Gabriel with a cheerful kindly face. He holds a scroll on which is written "Hail Mary", full of Grace; "The Lord is with thee!" Beside him stands Mary — (21) humbly attentive to the Angelic Salutation. This is followed by the Visitation, where Elizabeth, (22) inspired by the Holy Ghost, salutes Mary in her prophetic hymn as "the Mother of my Lord".

23. This being the beginning of the new Revelation, we see next to these the Jewish Church, the counterpart of the Christian Church which faces her across the porch, but with her eyes blindfolded, her standard broken, her book of the law and prophecy closed and fallen to the ground denoting that her task was ended

having "brought us to Christ". This was a favourite
subject in the middle ages as may be seen at Strasburg as well as in other churches, with sometimes
the following inscriptions: The Church says "With
the blood of Christ I conquer". The Synagogue
says "With the blood of Christ I am blinded".

Now begins again the row of smaller figures.
First as types of the unreadiness of the Jewish
Church to recognize our Lord, stand the Five
Foolish Virgins, 24, 25, 26, 27, 28 in varied
but graceful attitudes of despair, or in a half
waking half sleeping state, their gifts wasted,
their lamps extinguished or broken, shut out from
the Marriage supper. These are by far the best
statues artistically, both in design and execution very superior to all the rest. Taken in
conjunction with the Seven Liberal Arts which
follow them, we may look on the whole line as
typical of the use and misuse of the new teaching, *these*, with their gifts and illuminating
powers wasted, *those*, fostered by the Church
to God's greater glory. In the middle ages
the Church was the great instructor of the nations.
The scientists of those days were almost always
found in her cloisters and colleges. A knowledge of the Liberal Arts was above all indis-
pensable to the architect of a cathedral, and
without them no portrait of human life would
be considered complete.

Their presence in this porch typifies the Redeemed life of man.

The Seven Liberal Arts or Free Arts (so named because the Free born only were allowed to pursue them) are the foundation of all secular science. —

29. First stands Grammatica, two boys are under her tuition, the diligent one reads in a book, the lazy one receives wholesome chastisement with a rod held by Grammatica.

30. Next to knowing how to *read* comes the art of *Sound speech.* Rhetorica holds in her hand golden coins — the flowing of gold typifies usually fluent and well-timed speech, and St. Chrysostom on account of his persuasive eloquence was named "Golden-mouthed". But to this gift must be added sound reasoning power;

31. so Dialectica next appears in the act of demonstration, showing on her extended fingers the logical proof of the truth of her assertions.

32. Next stands Geometria, the science of quantity, proportion and mensuration, holding a square, compasses and measure in her hands.

33. Musica — the scientific arrangement of sounds, comes next in order — striking a bell with a hammer and attentively listening to the vibrations of sound.

34. Astronomia now lifts science from more immediate and more personal, to more abstract

2*

and higher use, and with quadrant and glass is occupied in examining the Heavens and Inanimate Nature.

35. Medica denotes the study of the healing powers of nature as applied to the relief of humanity. She holds a retort or bottle.

The figure of Medica brings us back to the s. west corner of the porch, and here, with their faces to the Church and their backs to the World we find, corresponding in position to "the World", its allurements and its bitternesses, two of the Saints of God, truest anti-types of the World, the Flesh and the Devil, bright examples of the fullest dedication and devotion of all the good gifts of Beauty, Great Station and Power, Intellect and Cultivation, to the sole service of God.

36. in St. Margaret, virgin martyr, who tramples upon the Dragon the emblem of sin and evil — and 37 St. Katharine, noble virgin of Alexandria, from her earliest youth devoted to study, and who by her clear and eloquent exposition of her faith brought over to Christianity the learned doctors sent to persuade her to abjure it.

Before proceeding with the great history of Redemption which we are studying we must here pause to examine a most interesting group of figures, each about a foot high that are clustered together in the niche forming the pedestal which supports St. Katharine.

A man wearing the dress of an artist points to a scroll on which we read "Johannes Heber". Next him a ³/₄ length figure wears the cloak of the order of St. Dominic, and places his hand on a scroll which is held by an angel who looks toward the entrance. This angelic teaching indicates the preaching of the Gospel strengthened by heavenly influences. St. Dominic we must remember founded the Order of Preaching Friars. With the other hand the Dominican also points to the name of "Johannes Heber". Under his left arm peers out a friendly face, and he also points to the same name. Two rather mutilated figures seem to be studying a book.

Now it seems indisputable that the artist-figure in this group is the portrait of the sculptor of the surrounding figures, and that the friar represents the designer.

From old documents it is proved that in 1238 A. D. about fifty years before the erection of this portion of the Minster, Count Conrad the 1ˢᵗ had bestowed on the Dominicans a fine site for a monastery in the town of Freiburg, still occupied by their church and convent. To this order we doubtless owe the idea of the beautiful lesson of the porch; for though the laity were active and skilful in execution, the theological teaching of the sculptures would certainly emanate from the cloister.

Besides the artist Johannes Heber above named, it is very interesting to find the commemoration of two other workers at the Minster, though they are in places very easily overlooked. Beneath the kneeling Kings, or Wise Men is a group of small figures one bearing on a scroll the name of "Tomas Kobell".

Under the pedestal of the angel Gabriel another small figure has the name of "Mathe Gall" written on his scroll.

Thus we learn with friendly interest who were the designer, the artist, and their assistants, to whom we owe our gratitude for their beautiful and instructive work.

The Great West Entrance.

AND now standing before the massive double doors that will by-and-by admit us to the interior of the Minster, we find, placed upon the centre pillar of the archway that foundation-pillar of the Redemption of Man, that "most beloved Lady" to whom this church is dedicated; an expressive and beautiful statue, holding on her left arm the Infant Jesus, while with her right she offers Him a bunch of roses. Beside these figures grow, on one side a rose, and on the other a palm-tree. In the picture language of the Church Mary is called "the Mystic Rose"

and Jesus — the Rose of Sharon. In the Lesson
chosen for the Festival of the Assumption of the
B. V. Mary we read "She grew up as a mighty
palm in Cades, and as a rose-plant in Jericho".

Beneath this figure we see the Prophet Ezekiel
who sits asleep, representing thus his Vision which
he records in the 44ᵗʰ Ch. in his own prophetical
book 2. V. "Then said the Lord unto me : This
gate shall be shut, it shall not be opened and
no man shall enter by it, because the Lord God
of Israel hath entered in by it; therefore shall it
be shut." — Which prophecy relates to the perpetual Virginity of the B. V. Mary.

Now we will study the actual work of the
Redemption of Man by Christ — from the time
of his birth on earth to the gathering round His
throne of glory of all His redeemed in Heaven,
represented in the tympanum of the arch by four
tiers of multitudinous sculptured figures of small
size which demand, and will repay, a lengthy
and careful investigation.

We commence at the south corner of the
lowest tier, with the scene of the Nativity, opening
the story of Christ's earth life. To the right is
the Virgin reclining on a bedstead caressing the
Infant Whom she lifts from a manger. Over them
are three attendant angels. One swings a censer,
and another holds a candelabra; at the head of the
bed the ox and ass eat hay from the manger,

St. Joseph leans upon his staff at the foot of the bed, near him another angel shows the approaching shepherds a shield on which is written "I bring you glad tidings". Some sheep feed among plants in the corner.

The next group brings us at once to the Passion. Christ stands bound to a pillar, stripped of His garments and scourged. In the left corner we see Judas, hanging from the branch of a tree — the thirty pieces of silver falling out of his hand, while above in the boughs two devils are carrying off his soul spitted on a stick! This completes line the 1ˢᵗ.

Separated from this by a thin layer of clouds, two angels, at right and left proclaim the day of judgment. On the left side the Just seem to rise with alacrity and joy hastily clothing themselves with the good actions done in their lifetime, to stand unabashed before the throne of God. To a careless observer this is a drolly realistic scene, but it is intensely typical. — One man is drawing on a huge pair of blackleather boots, others are slipping on a shirt, or trowsers. Bishops and Religious rise ready clothed. Peace is reflected on all these faces, and an angel stands to defend them from an ungainly figure, a kind of satyr who endeavours to approach them holding a large cauldron and a scull, signifying by this the entire delivrance of the Just from all

further attacks of Satan, and of Death. To the
right of the scene are crowds of the Lost, on
whose woeful faces we read their wretched doom.
These rise with difficulty and pain half crushed
by their heavy tombs.

Between the Blessed and the Lost stands a
tall angel, before whose feet a deformed and
dwarfed figure with the head of an ape and
eagle's claws for hands, stands with his hands
raised, and clasped as if in earnest prayer. This
alludes to the text — "the Devils also believe,
and tremble".

Now to this figure is attached an interesting
reminiscence of the old annals of Freiburg.

In the middle ages (as indeed to some extent
even to these days) all young apprentices learn
their trade by working from town to town during
a given number of years, before they come to be
enrolled in their respective guilds at home, and
to verify their account of their travels they had
to answer certain crucial questions as to the
peculiarities of the towns they had visited.

One of these questions was to this effect:
"Where have you seen the Devil saying his
prayers?" The "Praying Devil" was a distinctive
mark of a sojourn in Freiburg.

Across the whole width of this picture of
the Lost is a rope which is twisted round every
neck in the string of Lost souls. A hideous

devil holds the end, and by it drags them into a furnace where jeering devils mock them from below.

The crowning centrepiece filling the point of the arch is a Crucifixion, the culminating point of the Redemption. "God is the Lord by Whom we escape Death."

The cross is a tree, stripped of boughs and leaves, expressing thus the deep truth that, as in Paradise Satan reigned upon the fatal Tree in the midst of the Garden, so on the Tree of Calvary in the centre of the Garden of the World was he vanquished — as says the old Latin hymn:

"And Christ hath reigned from the Tree." The withered and bare tree alludes to Is. 2. v. 1. "There shall come forth a Rod out of the Stem of Jesse and a Branch and shall grow out of his roots."

The descendants of David and Jesse were, at the time our Lord was born of their direct Line of the B. V. Mary, living in obscurity among the handi-craftsmen of the land — and yet from this apparently dry Stem and Root sprang forth the Branch and the Rod of the new Creation.

At the foot of the cross is the scull — Death overcome by the Cross. Above it a pele-can feeding her nestlings, according to the tradition that she recalls them to life by feeding them with her own life-blood — most touching

symbol of the great Sacrament of our Salvation,
the life-giving Sacrament of the Altar.

To the right and left of the cross stand the
B. V. Mary, St. John the Evangelist, St. Longinus
the Centurion, — first of the gentile world to
testify publicly "This man was the Son of God",
— and a number of bishops, kings and apostles,
seated enthroned among the clouds apparently
in animated conversation as intercessors and
judges, according to the promise "at the Regenera-
tion .. ye shall sit upon thrones judging the
twelve tribes of Israel". Above all, at the point
of the arch, sits our Blessed Lord upon His
throne of Judgment, showing still the glorious
Wounds in Hands, Feet and Side, with which
He ascended into Heaven. Beside His throne
kneel His blessed Mother — the Fount of the
Incarnation — and St. John the Baptist the Precursor, and greatest of the Old Dispensation. Four
angels carry the Insignia of His Victory and two
proclaiming angels stand above with a seventh
angel who holds the Sun, fit emblem of the
Everlasting Light, the Sun of Righteousness.

Most fit surrounding to these central scenes
of our Redemption, most fit surrounding for the
throne of the Lord of Heaven and Earth, let
us now observe that each hollow of the great
portal arch moulding is enriched by sculptured
figures, one above another, of prophets and priests,

Kings, Heroes and Angels, the Hierarchy of Heaven, the Church of the Redeemed, the memorial of those by whom great deeds were done, to whom great promises and revelations were made, or who were instruments in God's hands for the advancement of his Kingdom.

To the right we begin with (1) Adam, (2) Abel with his Lamb of Sacrifice, (3) Seth in attitude of prayer, from whom descended the Hebrew nation and consequently the Messiah also, (4) Noah with the Ark —. (5) Melchizedek with bread and wine, foreshowing the New Dispensation, (6) Abraham with the Sacrificial knife, seizing a ram by its horn. (7) Isaac with a faggot of wood, (8) Jacob with a ladder. (9) Judah from whom descended the Shiloh. At the top we begin on the opposite side of the arch with (10) Moses the Leader with his Rays of glory, (11) Aaron "the called of God". (12) Eleazar his successor, (13) Caleb, with the clusters of Eschol grapes. (14) Joshua the Conqueror of Canaan, (15) Gideon with a fleece, (16) Deborah "who judged Israel", and thus at (17) we find Cain — with his unaccepted offering, first cause of that division among mankind spoken of in Holy Scripture as "the Sons of God" and the "Children of Men", explained by St. Augustine as the Church and the World, of whom Abel and Cain are the types, and (18) Eve "the Mother of all living" faces Adam the first man.

The second hollow contains 16 kings of
Judah, ancestors of our Lord, with crowns and
sceptres, and robed in ermine. At the point of
the arch stands our Lord as King of Kings with
Imperial insignia of Sword and Orb.

The 3ᵈ space contains the prophets from
Isaiah to Malachi. Jonah forming the centre-
point of the arch, coming out of the whale's
mouth not only a prophet, but a type, pointed
to by our Lord Himself as foreshowing His
burial and resurrection on the third day. The other
prophets represented are Jeremiah, Daniel, Baruch,
Hosea, Amos, Obadiah, Micah, Nahum, Habbakkuk,
Zephaniah, Haggai and Zachariah. Ezekiel,
completing the 16 prophets, we have already
seen on another part of the doorway beneath
the feet of the central Madonna and Child.

The 4ᵗʰ and inner hollow of the arch is filled
with angels some holding crowns, some with
censers, symbolizing the glory and joy of the
Great Day of the Lord.

And thus we have followed and completed
the great drama of The World and the Creation
of God from its opening to its final goal in
glory.

Let us now examine more minutely a few architectural details connected with the great portal-

arch, the jambs of which we see are composed
of three pillars, each composed of a cluster
of three, united under one capital or shrine,
deeply emblematic of the doctrine of the Holy
Trinity, the base and support of all faith.

It is on the top of these capitals that stand
the figures of the Church — the Magi — the
Salutation, the Incarnation, etc., already mentioned at page 25.

The main outline of the arch rises from the
stone step, and continues without break till the
lines unite at the top of the arch, and though
the smaller clusters of pillars may give an impres-
sion that they support the main arch, it is not
so in reality.

Though it is true that the great Story of the
Redemption has been fully displayed before our
eyes, there are still many very interesting episodes
in Church history, placed to complete the wonderful lesson of the porch and teach the people
from books of stone when other books were
none, or hardly to be obtained. — And for the
first series of these we must rather closely examine
the groups of very small figures, enshrined within
the capitals of the six clusters of pillars forming
the great arch. The first we see point out Holy
Baptism as the *Seal*, and Holy Martyrdom as

the SEED of the Church; these stand, the first
beneath the figure of the Church (as the first
fruit, or beginning of the Christian life), and the
martyrdom beneath the other figures, as far as
the statue of Mary, the Root of the Church in
the Incarnation.

Under the figure of the Church then, we
see a monk or priest leading two boys by the
hand towards their royal parents; the queen
kneels to receive them. Near her stands a man
with a ducal or Phrygian cap, who may be taken
to represent the sponsor. — An inscription
behind the priest says "Hic reddit pueros im-
mersos", "He gives back the baptized boys".
In the corner we see two men dressed as pilgrims
who kneel before a throne and receive a crown
from the person seated thereon who is attended
by another figure. — This doubtless shows the
life of the two baptized boys, as Christian
pilgrims receiving from God their crown of glory
before His throne. In the corner opposite this,
stands Christ sending forth His apostles to teach
and "Baptize all Nations".

Beneath the three Magi we see the Martyrdom
of Sᵗ John the Baptist. In front King Herod and
Herodias are seated at their banquet surrounded by
courtiers and musicians; in front of the table cloth
is a small figure swathed in a tight fitting dress,
walking on its hands, feet upwards. — This is

3*

evidently the young daughter of Herodias dancing,
or rather "posturing" before the king, exactly after
the manner of Eastern athletes and Asiatic jug-
glers and dancers male and female to this day,
whose dress of fine soft muslin is exactly the
costume of this figure. At the side we see the prison
of John. At an upper window Herodias' daughter
waits to receive the head, and below at another
window we see St. John, at whose head an executioner aims a blow with his sword. — Between
these two groups is seen a servant with shorn
head and a cowl, bearing the head on a great
dish to place it before the queen.

In the smaller shrines on each side of the
doorway are angels, one holding "the wedding
garment", and one swinging a censer. Both
denoting the glorification of the Martyrs in
Heaven.

The next shrine depicts the martyrdom of
St. Bartholomew.

On the left sits a king beside a pillar, on
which is the image of the Bull Apis, he is
evidently commanding a man who stands before
him to worship this heathen Deity, which the
man refuses to do. On the other side an executioner proceeds to flay alive a man whom by
this we recognize as St. Bartholomew. A man stands
over the executioner urging him on in his ghastly
work by flourishing over him a small scourge.

Into this man's ear a devil is whispering, while
an angel strengthens the martyr to endure his
agonies.

Beneath the shrine of Mary saying "Be it unto
me" we find our Lord surrounded by his apostles
after the Resurrection and directing St. Thomas to
"reach hither" his hand and lay his finger in the
Sacred wounds, thus giving assurance that the
Flesh of His risen and glorified Body is that
same Flesh which He took of His Blessed Mother.

Behind our Lord stands a woman with a
ring on her breast, denoting the Church His Bride
born from His wounded side as Eve was born
from the wounded side of Adam.

Next we see the attempted martyrdom of
St. John the Evangelist placed in a cauldron of
boiled oil at the port Lateran at Rome, while a
royal couple stand by, ordering the execution; and
beyond this is the death of St. Peter who was crucified head downwards not judging himself worthy:

> "He who had thrice denied his Lord
> "The very death He died, to die."

In the corner stands a queen with an attendant
lady, probably converts, who cheer and comfort him.

————

From the time the Minster was built till
the beginning of this century the whole wall of
the porch was covered with frescoes — from

the upper range of seats to the base of the statues we have been describing. These paintings illustrated the Life of Christ, and each event in that life was alternated by its prototype in Old Testament history. It speaks not well for modern Freiburg that so valuable and instructive an example of old art and piety should have been allowed to fade away, and no attempt be made to retain or to restore it — the more so as a very epidemic of the Alt-Deutsch Decorative Art has broken out and covered the house-fronts of private individuals in all the old German towns and especially so in Freiburg, showing that there are still hands ready to perform the work, if hearts were but willing.

Indeed sufficient traces of outline and of colour are still remaining to guide to a careful restoration, and a very minute account of the frescoes has been left by Doctor Schreiber, who saw them in 1820 before they were obliterated, and who tells that each New Testament subject was placed between two from the Old Testament, thus:

Beginning on the right side of the great door with our Lord's triumphal entry into Jerusalem, on one side was David's victory over Goliath and on the other Judith's victory over Holophernes.

Next came the institution of the Eucharist

flanked by its types — the gathering of the Manna
and the offering by Melchizedek.

The betrayal by Judas typified by the trea-
cherous murder of Abner by Joab, and the
seizure of Jonathan by Tryphon as his prisoner.
Christ bears His cross up Calvary — Isaac carries up Mount Moriah the wood for his own
sacrifice — the Widow of Zarepta "gathers a
few sticks that she and her son may eat and die".

Jesus crucified is supported on one side by Isaac
kneeling on the altar-pyre, and Moses lifting up
the Serpent in the Wilderness, upon a cross.

The burial of Christ has on one side, Joseph
let down into a pit by his brothers, and on the
other, Jonah swallowed by the whale. Christ
delivers the spirits in prison, David delivers
Israel, and Samson carries off the gates of
Gazah. Christ rises from the bonds of the grave,
— Samson bursts the green withies that bound
him. Jonah is cast up alive on land by the whale
on the third day.

On one side the Ascension of Christ, and
facing it the Assumption of our Blessed Lady.

The names of the original teacher of the
people who designed this, and of the painter
who so well carried out his thought are now
known only to Him for the spread of whose
kingdom they laboured. — But on two boards·
hanging in the porch up to 1878 (since removed)

are portraits of Jacob Mock, Professor of Medicine, and of his wife Maria Salome Hermann from Thann, who in 1604 A. D. caused these frescoes to be restored. He died 28. February 1616 and Maria his wife followed him on the 11. December in the same year.

Will Freiburg never again find a loving couple, zealous and united in good works, to join in restoring these ancient glories of that Minster of which Freiburg is still so justly proud, and in making her walls again cry aloud to the entering people the great truths of their Salvation-Story?

But another point remains to be noticed. Looking up to the Groined roof where the painting, less exposed to the weather still survives, we see in each corner the four principal prophets and in each panel an evangelist; round the centre-rosette are four proclaiming angels, to N. S. E. and W.; fitting culmination to the great history that in all its length is depicted round the wondrous porch below and descriptive of the great Mission of Christ's Church and Her obedience to the order of Her Founder: *Teach all Nations.*

Inside the Minster.

ENTERING the Minster through the great west doorway let us first turn and look behind us,

and see, on the great centre pillar of the door
arch a very beautiful statue of the B. V. Mary
with the Infant Jesus; the drapery has been
gilt and coloured. This is accounted the finest
statue in the Cathedral. At the same level, in
each angle of the tower-wall is an attendant
angel bearing a candelabra. Far. above their
heads the nave is crossed by a richly carved-gallery
of stone forming the open side of the first floor
of the tower — over the open porch, and under
the clock and bell-chambers. From no place
is a more beautiful view to be obtained of the
whole interior, and from no spot can any procession or ceremony be seen to better advantage.

Near the entrance door let us remark a very
beautiful and elaborate piece of modern metal-
work in iron, bronze, and brass, serving as a
bénitier.

The Painted Glass.

THE windows of the Minster date chiefly from
the end of the 13th and beginning of the 14th
centuries, when through the liberality and devotion of the faithful the windows were entirely
filled with painted glass of the greatest richness
and variety. Each Freiburghian trade-guild presented a window distinguished by its own guild
mark. Nobles and burghers vied with each other

in these offerings and the varied coats of arms
show how various were the donors.

In 1347 Johann Snewelin, Chevalier and
Mayor bequeathed his finest steed and trappings
to pay for a window.

Too much alas! of the original glass has fallen
a prey to the ravages of time and of modernizers.
But a great deal remains intact of both the
mullions and the glass, and much very good
restoration was effected when in 1818 A. D. the
glass from the Chapel of St. Mauritius in Constance was purchased, as also in 1820 when a
further purchase of glass from the Dominican
Friary in Freiburg of the same date as the
Minster, enabled the windows to be replaced almost as at the beginning.

In fact the windows are at this day nearly
perfect, though the different dates at which they
were placed prevent any great uniformity of style.

The interior of the Minster is entirely surrounded by painted glass windows, those at the
west end being two very perfect and beautiful
rose, or wheel windows.

Each of these is divided into 16 compart-
ments. On the s. west is depicted the culture
of vines, that of corn on the other. The
pruning-knife on one, the mill wheel on the
other, show them to have been the offerings of
the guilds of vine dressers and of millers. Most

beautiful are these when seen in front of a setting sun, leading the mind up from the act of
devotion of these labouring men of old, to the
glorious Sacrament which is typified by Corn
and Wine.

South Windows.

ON the south side the 1ˢᵗ *window* is embel-
lished with four tall full length figures. St. *Peter*,
holding the Keys of Heaven, St. *Afra*, the first
Christian Martyr of Germany, burnt alive
at Augsburg A. D. 304. Her altar-tomb is to
this day in Augsburg Minster. In her hand is
always placed a box, supposed to contain her
offering of her own ashes. St. *Mary Magdalene*
holding the box of precious ointment — round
and under her feet demon-faces typify the former
sinful life she had led. St. *John* the Evangelist
holds a shield on which is depicted his Eagle.

Above these figures are medallions illustrative
chiefly of the Passion of Christ, except in one
striking instance, which carries us back to the
days of chivalry; the Church is . represented
riding upon a warhorse which is a strange
amalgamation of the four evangelistic symbols,
its head composed of four faces: the bull, the
lion, the eagle and the angel. The four feet
continue the idea, one being human, one cloven,

one a paw and one a talon. — On this apocalyptic beast sits the Church, crowned, holding a
banner and a chalice, and fighting, lance in rest,
against the Synagogue, who, blindfolded and
riding upon an ass, holds in one hand a broken
standard and in the other a ram's head, and is falling backwards conquered before the Church.

In the lower portion of this window, which
was the gift of the guild of miners — the original men of Freiburg (which at its first beginning was founded and inhabited by miners only)
we see a representation of men working in the
adit of a mine, and smelting the ore. The
miners of the Black Forest were, of course, related
to the founders of the Minster. — Above the
painting is an inscription.

2nd *window*. S. side. The great central figure
is St. Christopher bearing the Infant Christ on
his shoulders across the Rhine, which is represented
as full of aquatic monsters and fish. Around
it are smaller scenes representing the Passion, from
the Last Supper to the Entombment. This window
was given by the guild of bootmakers, denoted
by the painting of a boot in one corner.

The Legend of Christopher (Christ-bearer)
is a very poetical story. Proud of his colossal
size (12 ells) Christopher vowed that he would
serve no master until he should find one stronger than himself, and therefore refused the soli-

— 49 —

citations of a good hermit to join the Christians
and be baptized. — The hermit, however, per-
suaded him to devote his size and strength to
the glory of God by carrying pilgrims across
the Rhine, and to this he consented, supporting
himself against the stream by a staff, which was
a whole uprooted fir-tree.

One stormy night a little child came to
him, and earnestly petitioned that he might be
carried across the river. The good-natured
giant placed the child on his shoulder and started.
But with every step he took, the child grew
heavier and heavier, till in the middle of the
river Christopher nearly sank beneath his burden.
"Say," cried he, "how is it that thou little child,
though growing no larger, hast crushed me by
thy weight? what and who art thou who hast
overpowered the giant Christopher?"

The child replied: „Thou didst boast O giant,
that thou wouldst serve no master till thou
shouldst find a stronger than thyself — fall on
thy knees, then, and worship Me, for I am Jesus,
Lord of Heaven and Earth, thy Master and
thy Saviour."

And from that hour Christopher became a
devoted servant of the Most High God.

Above the figure of the saint are two medallions; Jesus on the Mount of Olives, and the
Church enthroned bearing chalice and sceptre.

Window third has our Blessed Lady in the
centre, with St. Andrew on her right hand; and
on the left are two figures representing the donors
of the glass, their names written on a shield are
Adelheid and Frantz Tulenhaupt. Above these
the legend of St. Nicholas fills the remainder.
We see him throwing through a window a bag
of gold to form a dowry for some poor girls
whose father had abandoned them to a life of
shame, being unable to keep them from star-
vation. Then as Bishop of Myra we see St.
Nicholas restoring to life the three children of
a poor widow, who had been seized by a cruel
creditor, killed and salted. down for food. A
portion of this having been served at the Bishop's
table, it was revealed to him that it was human
flesh, and tracing the remainder he was miraculously empowered to restore the children alive
to their mother. From this legend comes the
especial patronage of young children by St. Nicholas. It is he who is thought to bring their
Christmas gifts and joys under the well known
name of Sant'i Claus.

Again he is invoked as a special protector
from thieves.

A story is told of a Jew who placed a picture
of St. Nicholas in his house as a guardian of
his goods. — Nevertheless thieves broke in, and
robbed him. — In this window we see the Jew

flogging the picture of St. Nicholas. St. Nicholas appears to him, and directs him how to detect the thieves and recover his goods, which having done, the Jew embraces Christianity under his guidance.

The medallions on this window represent Christ as King supported by two angels, and two other subjects not very recognizable — a man seems to be receiving a mission from Christ. — Beneath is a coat of arms. Three leaves on one stalk, on a mound, with the inscription many times repeated "Dieselmuot". This is the name of a large iron - mine, worked in 1343 A. D. The window was probably offered by those who owned or worked this mine.

Window 4. The B. V. Mary holding in her left hand a book, and on her right hand the Child Jesus over Whom is a dove. The smaller subjects are nine Martyrs, viz: Vincentius, burnt with torches — Theudibert Bishop — whose eyes were put out 304 A. D., Ignatius of Antioch — devoured by lions., Alexander of the Theban Legion 302 A. D. pierced by swords, a male figure above whom is wrongly written "Margaret", St. Katharine, with the wheel, martyred 307 A. D., St. Anastasia. In the upper part of the window the Blessed Virgin in glory surrounded by angels — the Nativity, and the Adoration of the Magi.

Window 5. Contains only the four Evangelists.
Window 6. Displays the conquest of the

great serpent the Devil, by St. Michael. Next to that is the day of Judgment. — Our Lord seated on a throne, on one side of His head is a lily, on the other a flaming sword. — Two angels with trumpets summon the dead; right and left are scrolls with "Stand up, ye dead to judgment" in Latin and in German. Beneath, the dead are rising, devils and angels are claiming their own. Below, the risen Christ appears to Mary Magdalene. — The Ascension — showing only the Lord's feet below a cloud and his foot prints upon the mountain top, round which stand the apostles. The Crucifixion with St. Mary and St. John and lastly, portraits of the donors of this window.

At the time of the alteration of the Minster the upper corner of this window was built over and darkened. This defect was at the same date concealed with great ingenuity and good taste, the heavy folds of a crimson curtain being so painted that it appears to be the sole cause of the onesidedness and darkening of the corner.

———

Now let us return to the western door and start anew from the northwestern corner beside the rose window.

Window 1 was an offering made by the guild of brewers, as we see from the beer-pitchers and measures in the corner. In the upper compartment is the suffering Saviour with scourges, and a chalice out of which rise the nails of the three glorious wounds. In a medallion St. Peter opens the doors of the Church with a silver key, and the door of Heaven with a golden one. In the next medallion is the Church seated as a queen, sceptre in hand, and holding a muscleshell, emblem of Baptism.

The large figures (restored) are St. Lawrence with a grid-iron, St. Mary and St. Nicholas.

Window 2. God the Father, the Son and the Holy Ghost, to Whom the Blessed Virgin Mary is presenting⸱ those people who are under her protection. — In front is the chalice with three nails, — above is the crown of thorns, behind are the cross, the lance, the scourge and rope.

Underneath is a figure of the Blessed Virgin enthroned under a canopy of state — her arms are outstretched, and near her two crowned figures appear to take refuge with her. This window is the gift of the guild of bakers as we see by the representation of a "Bretzel" the Christmas loaf eaten and given by every one at Freiburg at that season ∞ in this form.

St. Katharine noble virgin of Alexandria who was killed by the Emperor Maximin the 2ᵈ, or Maxentius — about the year 307, is the Patron Saint of bakers and the lower half of this window is devoted to her story. Here she is seen converting to the faith the wife of the Roman governor of Alexandria when she visited her in prison, and for this she was condemned to be broken on a wheel, but the instrument of torture was struck by lightning and destroyed. In the next compartment St. Katharine and her Roman convert receive two crowns from the hands of Christ.

The learned men of the great school of Alexandria were then commissioned to reason and persuade St. Katharine to renounce the Christian faith, instead of which the result was, that Katharine, by her eloquence, her excellent powers of argument, and the intensity of her convictions converted to the faith the whole school of philosophers, at which the Roman procurator was so incensed, that he drove the whole body of them into a church, including his own wife with St. Katharine, and setting fire to it consumed all within its walls, except St. Katharine who escaped, but was soon afterwards seized and beheaded. St. Katharine is throughout distinguished by her violet mantle while the Roman lady is robed in crimson; and it is due to the incident of her being thus partially baked to death that she was selected to be Patroness of the guild of bakers.

The inroads of the Saracens made Alexandria in later years an unsafe resting-place for the body of so great a Saint, and St. Helena the mother of Constantine having erected a convent on Mount Sinai before her death in 328, the body of St. Katharine was transported by angels from Alexandria and deposited within the convent of Mount Sinai, where her relics are still preserved. This translation of St. Katharine is depicted on the last medallion of this window.

It is St. Katharine of Alexandria who is represented in so many beautiful pictures as the espoused of the Infant Christ.

In her youth when much pressed to select a husband befitting her noble birth and great position she always replied that she had found no prince powerful or noble enough for her to wed. At that time a vision was vouchsafed her of the Saviour on His mother's knee holding out to her the ring of espousal. From that hour she received the permanent mark of a ring on her finger, similar to the stigmata afterwards vouchsafed to St. Francis of Assisi, and devoted her whole life to the Christian cause saying she had found at last a bridegroom worthy of her love.

Window 3, is the offering of the guild of farriers and blacksmiths, and tells the story of Saint Eligius their Patron. Among some beautiful geometrical patterns are representations of the Almighty holding two crowns, of Christ — crucified — of S.S. Peter and Paul, S.S. Mary and

John — the Annunciation and Salutation, and of St. Eligius in the act of healing miraculously a wounded horse, with many emblems of the arts of healing and metal-working or farriership — as forge, anvil, pincers, nails, hammer, the twisted serpents of Esculapius — the cup of healing &c. &c.

Window 4, the gift of the tailors' guild, is chiefly devoted to the Assumption of Mary, over whose head some angels hold a crown of glory, and others the garments of righteousness — below is the death of Mary, surrounded by the apostles; — and three large single figures, of St. Mary, St. Katharine and St. Barbara.

A large pair of tailor's shears denotes the guild.

WINDOW 5. The B. V. Mary enthroned — her head crowned by seven doves denoting the seven gifts of the Holy Spirit. On her knee is the Infant Jesus. Jesus on a cross surmounted by a pelican, His emblem, beside Him stands His mother. Beyond are Solomon, David and smaller figures of Bishops and Deacons, angels and a lioness with five cubs. On this window is inscribed "Nellins Frond" — a mine mentioned in the same archives of 1343 with that of Dieselmuot already referred to —. The window is evidently given by the workers of this mine.

Window 6. St. Margaret and the dragon; Christ &c. Glass, modern, by Helmle Sen'.

Windows in the Transepts.

THE Romanesque portions of these windows
are the oldest portion of the Minster. — On the
north side are depicted the seven corporal works
of Mercy. — On the south side — Christ, the
Alpha and Omega, enthroned. — In the window
beneath the singers' gallery is the figure of an
apostle; on that nearest the entrance to the
choir are traces of Renaissance work.

Facing these, beside the south door and near
the entrance to the sacristy is an exquisite
little window of the very best modern glass from
the studio of Helmle and Merzweiler placed in
the Minster in 1883 by an Englishman, Colonel
Roberts, who has made Freiburg his adopted
home, and who is greatly respected and beloved
by the Freiburghers, although he does not belong
to the Roman obedience, and whose offering
of this exquisite window, placed to the memory
of two of his children, has been accepted by the
Cathedral authorities. — It represents the two
great Saints of England — St. George, her Patron, holding the banner of England on his breast,
and the red rose on his shield. St. Thomas of
Canterbury bears a lily and the palm branch
of martyrdom. Conventional corn-flowers, for
Germany, and roses, for England, — fill the cor-

ners. Beneath is the memorial inscription to the children.

After the placing of the above window, a powerful field glass, brought to the donor's notice a very singular coincidence — namely that, in the central cleres tory window over the High altar, St. George and St. Thomas of Canterbury have already for hundreds of years stood side by side in Freiburg Minster, St. George being at the time of the construction of that window, the Patron of Freiburg.

The Frescoes.

THE mural space above the great east arch of the nave was in the year 1877 made over to the painter Louis Seitz of Rome who undertook the partial renovation and completion of an almost obliterated fresco, bearing the date of 1547 A. D. This again had been painted over another whose traces show it to have belonged to the 14th century, both having been destroyed by damp or the bad material of the plaster background. — The subject is throughout the same as before, and the Madonna is almost like a copy from the great tryptich over the High altar. — Mary crowned by the Holy Trinity.

Under a commission from the administrators of the founder's fund Seitz was employed to

cover the ground occupied by the vanished frescoes, and all competent judges have pronounced
that few living artists could have so well har-
monized the ancient style with modern taste in
church decoration. The colours are perhaps at
present a trifle too aggressive among the chas-
tened tints and subdued lights of this essentially
reverend building, but time and the dust of
centuries will do their softening work, and account must be taken of the great height at which
it stands, and the strong deep red of all the
surrounding stone.

The centre of the picture is the B. V. Mary
enveloped in a flowing mantle of blue. She
sits, an embodiment of matronly dignity and
modesty and motherly love, bending towards Her
Son, Who sits upon the same throne holding
over her with one hand a crown and with the
Book of Life resting upon His knees. Behind
these central figures extends a drapery of beautiful design held suspended by two angels, and a
rainbow forms an arch over them. The sky is
studded with stars and the steps of the throne are
strewn with red, yellow and white roses — sweet
remembrances of the Rosary. On the right and
left of the throne stand as it were as witnesses
of the heavenly act St. Conrad Bishop of
Constance, (of the ancestral family of our own
beloved Queen Victoria) St. Bernard, St. Lambert

and St. Alexander of the Theban legion — the two latter the glorious Patrons of Freiburg. — Two kneeling angels present a crown and sceptre, and the two low points of the arch are filled by angels swinging censers of incense. Above all is the text: "Ego dilecto meo et ad me conversio ejus."

Beside the altar of the Blessed Sacrament at the south east end of the nave is a beautifully executed life-sized full length fresco of our Blessed Lord. Painted by *Sebastian Luz* in 1868 in memory of Baronin A. von R . . . g, and above this is a greatly injured and half-effaced fresco of St. Martin dividing his cloak with a beggar at the gate of Amiens which, judging by the traces that can still be seen, must have been very effective and of good workmanship.

The Statues in the Nave.
The 12 Apostles.

On the pillars of the nave, and on the two forming the arch of the choir, are statues of the apostles of Christ standing on the decorated capitals, as on pedestals, surmounted by canopies. The statues are well designed, with bold outline and graceful draperies, but are not by the same hand as the statues of the porch. The old painting and gilding is still fresh enough to add greatly to their effect.

Beginning on the left hand St. Peter is well placed at the entrance of the church as the first among the apostles, holding the keys of the Kingdom of Heaven and pointing with one hand to Satan, or an Evil spirit writhing beneath his feet, and to the text: "The gates of Hell shall never prevail against thee."

St. Paul stands next, leaning on a sword, — the emblem of his martyrdom by beheading, in Rome. His expression of composure, yet of movement denotes him as the evangelist of the Gentile world.

St. Bartholomew, designated by the knife which tore off his skin.

St. Andrew has a small cross made of boughs in that form called the cross of St. Andrew, on which he suffered martyrdom.

St. Matthias elected to fill the room of Judas Iscariot. In his hand is a book wherein is written: "Thou hast hidden these things from the wise and prudent, and revealed them unto babes." The hatchet is his sign of martyrdom.

On the pedestals of these three apostles are coats of arms, doubtless those of the giver of these statues.

St. Jude, or Thaddeus has in his hand a broken club. — Among the Epistles there is a short one written by him. His festival is held conjointly with that of St. Simon on the 28th Oct. as tradition tells that they suffered martyrdom together. On this pedestal is an angel swinging a censer.

On the left hand choir-pillar stands St. Thomas holding a closed book to denote his entire acceptance of the faith without further questioning. His eyes are fixed upon the Saviour Who stands facing him on the right hand choir-pillar, holding aloft a cross and showing to Thomas His sacred wounds.

Next our Lord as in life he stood, here also stands St. John the Evangelist. His usual attribute, the eagle, is at his feet, with eyes according to the legend fixed on the sun, fitting type of him to whom was given the sight of the king in His glory and of the apocalyptic vision, some of the radiance of which seems to rest upon his bright golden hair.

St. James the Elder (or the Great) in pilgrim weeds, with staff, scrip and shallop shell. He travelled as far as Compostella in Spain carrying the Gospel tidings — and on his return to Jerusalem, was there beheaded by Herod.

St. James the Less, son of Alphaeus, is represented with a cudgel in his hand having been beaten to death.

On the same pedestal is placed St. Philip, because the pillar next following is entirely occupied by the pulpit with its canopy. —

St. Philip is a pleasing figure carrying a small

decorated cross, tradition saying that he also
suffered the death of crucifixion.

St. Matthew stands under a palm-tree holding
the book of his Gospel.

St. Simon Zelotes faces St. Jude, he carries a
saw, implement of his martyrdom.

It is seldom that "the Glorious Company of
the Apostles" are so accurately and so comple-
tely represented as in this Minster.

In the hand of, or beside each figure, is placed
an enormous wax-taper. These are lighted during
solemn vespers and benediction and on the greater
festivals such as the Christmas and much enhance the effect of the figures.

Berchthold the Fifth.

THE only monument of the old Dukes of Zähringen is one of Berchthold the 5th Duke, which
stands in a recess between two small mural
pillars against the south wall of the nave. It
is that of a man greatly above the average size,
with hands joined as in prayer. The extreme
simplicity of the costume, which is well preserved, marks its great antiquity. The plain hel-
met has no vizor, but has a very primitive
contrivance of an iron band over the chin which
can be pushed up to protect the mouth and nose.

4*

Over a tight fitting shirt of chain mail is drawn
a sleeved coat. His sword is girt on by a
leather belt and on his right side hangs a dag-
ger — both being fastened by a twisted chain
upon his breast.

His feet rest on a lion, usual symbol of
knightly valour. This statue long stood over the
grave where Berchthold was laid, the last of
his race on Feb. 14. A. D. 1218.

But that was filled in about 1513, and the
great slab which had covered it was taken to
form a slab for the High altar.

Memorials of the Archbishops.

On the opposite side of the Minster against the
north wall in a recess between the lines of decorative pillars, similar to that occupied by Duke
Berchthold on the south side, is a noble marble
statue of the saintly and benevolent Doctor
Bernhard Boll, first Archbishop of Freiburg
from Oct. 11. 1827, till his death on March 6th,
1836, at the age of 80. — Born at Stuttgard in
1756 he became Abbot of the Bernardine Cloister of Salem, subsequently Professor of Philoso-
phy in the Freiburg University and Priest of
the Cathedral.

The statue of admirable workmanship, was
executed by A. Friedrich of Strasburg at the

expence of the Chapter, and is said to be a most
life-like portrait of this greatly beloved and
venerated Archbishop.

Near is the simple square of marble which
marks the grave of Archbishop Ignaz Demeter.
A short inscription records that he was Archbishop
and Metropolitan of Freiburg till March 21. 1842.
The grave of the 3ᵈ Metropolitan and Archbishop
is also marked by a similar square of marble in
front of the chapel of the Last Supper. — On
it flowers are always laid and renewed, and in
front of it stands a carpet and special priedieu
that passers-by may kneel and breath a prayer
for his repose in paradise. On the stone is inscribed Hermann Von Vicari, Archbishop, died
April 1868 — born May 13. 1773 at Aulendorf.

The Pulpit.

THE pulpit hewn from a single block of stone,
is the work of Jörg Kempf of Rhinek. It is
placed against a pillar of the south side of the
nave which is quite concealed by it and its
sounding board above. It is approached by some
stairs behind, the balustrade of which is an exquisite piece of carving, a wreath of angels' heads
and wings, roses and other flowers most intri-
cately entertwined.

The entrance to these stairs is protected by a

high gate of wrought iron, very old, and of very beautiful open design.

The support beneath the pulpit is one of the most interesting curiosities of the Minster, for the artist Jörg Kempf has represented himself — life size, as looking out of a sloping window in a turret staircase, such as we see to-day in many old Freiburg houses. He pushes open the window with one hand, and holds the implements of his craft in the other, the face is admirable and speaking, and every detail of the costume is as fresh as if carved yesterday.

The architecture of the window and the "bottle glass" panes of the open lattice are also interesting. Beneath we read in Latin that "With the help of God and his own genius and industry, this work was successfully completed by Jörg Kempf of Rhinek in the year 1561.

The Old Organ.

PERCHED on high, against the north wall of the nave to which it clings like a swallow's nest, supported only, apparently, by some richly gilt carved stone work, is the large organ — now called the old organ, since a more modern one has been placed in the choir.

The old organ was the gift of an English Baronet Sir John Sutton who having been some

years a resident at Kiedrich, near the Rhine
died there in June 1873. The memory of this
benefactor is perpetuated by an inscription placed
upon the organ itself. Made by Hockhois of
Brussels it was used for the first time on the
Feast of the Ascension 1871. It has 1500 pipes,
26 registers and two manuals — and its rich
tones prove sufficient for even the noble pro-
portions of this Cathedral.

The doors which cover it, and form with its
façade a beautiful tryptich, were, in accordance
with the will of the giver, painted in 1874 by
D' Martin in the later Gothic style and the
complete decoration was carried out by Wilhelm
Weber and J. Reichenstein.

At the time of the restoration an organ of
1818 was removed, it had but 500 pipes and
was supposed to have been built by Silbermann.
Records are preserved of still older organs.
According to the archives of 1503 the Chancellor
of the Minster ordered Master Martin Grünbach
of Ulm to build an organ with "hültzen Floutten".
The work was so well executed that the Magi-
strates of Freiburg were unanimous in present-
ing Master Martin with the Freedom of the City.

In the archives of the fabric of the Minster of
the date 1544, we find a notice concerning this
organ namely that Master Jergen Ebert organ-
builder of Raffenspurg was directed to supply the

organ with new works at a cost of 140 Gulden.
In 1545 and 46 the offerings of pilgrims amount-
ing to the sum of about 26 Gulden was expended
on repainting the figure of the Blessed Virgin
on this organ.   In all it cost 1,065 Gulden.

On the ledge of the parapet was inscribed:

Hostem quid stygium fugat, Organa quid pede sternit?
Virtus Davidis, Christi paræ et Mariæ.

O. L.

These lines allude to the dispelling of the
Evil spirit of Melancholy from the mind of Saul
by the skilful music of David, as also to the
Madonna on the organ who tramples the Evil
spirit beneath her feet.

Undoubtedly Grünbach's was not the first organ;
for Strasburg, our rival Minster, possessed one
as early as 1260 A. D. attributed to Ulrich
Engelbrecht; and in the year 757 the Emperor
Constantine the 5th presented the Frank King
Pepin with an organ furnished with bellows.
In the reign of Charlemagne an organ was placed
in the Cathedral of Aix la Chapelle, which con-
tained so many improvements that Pope John 8th
requested a German organ-builder might be sent
to Rome.   In the poem of "Titurel the Younger"
an organ is mentioned which was worked by a
windmill outside the church.   From the 10th
century organs became, in fact, very general,

though unwieldly and cumbersome in their construction. From the 15ᵗʰ century they began to be inclosed in wooden cases and highly ornamented.

Side Chapels and Altars of the Nave.

1. Grafen or Olivet Chapel.

CLOSE beside the north west entrance door of the Minster we find a deep recess fitted as a chapel. Up to the year 1829 this was a Mount of Olives shrine built up against the outer wall of the church, consisting of a rockery and group of figures in stone, which depicted our Lord's Agony in the Garden of Olives. This became a favourite place of interment for those nobles who could obtain that privilege (hence the name of Grafen-Capelle). Jörg Kempf, the artist of the pulpit executed the Olivet group in 1558, which date with his initials is recorded on the water spout.

But, in 1829, it was judged expedient to cut away the wall of the church and so enclose this chapel with a wall and windows thus embracing it into the body of the Minster. The work was carried out by the architect Frei — who supported the wall by pillars.

The glass is but indifferent and the colouring bad, the subjects are the unconsumed burning bush, seen by Moses before which he kneels.

Beneath is this inscription: "In the unconsumed
bush seen by Moses, perceive we Thy estimable
virginity, Oh mother of our Lord, our Intercessor."
On the other window is depicted David playing
the harp and singing the praises of God, with
this inscription from the 109th Ps.: "The Lord
said unto my Lord: Sit Thou at my Right Hand."

2. Chapel of the Last Supper.

FOLLOWING the north wall we come to a bay, or
recess, filled by a wonderful life-sized representation of the Last Supper and Institution of the
Holy Eucharist, backed by some exquisite glass
executed from old designs by Albert Dürer —
representing scenes from the Passion. This glass
was from the studio of the Brothers Helmle,
executed in 1826 and was an offering from the
Baron Louis Ferdinand Benedict von Reinach-
Werth, of the Johanniter Order (who died 1841)
to the memory of his parents and other relatives.

The recess beneath the glass which fills the
upper part of the wall — holds a stone table,
between which and the wall are seated the figures
of the Lord and His apostles. First our Lord,
in the centre, holding the Sacramental Cup. St.
John has thrown himself across His breast as if
asking the question "Who is it, Lord?"

On the other side sits St. Peter, his hands clasped
— gazing at the Lord — beyond on both sides

sit the remaining 10 apostles divided into groups
in a way most natural at the end of a repast —
some talk together, one is whispering into the
ear of a neighbour, in all there is the most life-
like variety of type and action, while the faces
are exactly such as may be seen in any collection
of peasants and artizans — all look like portraits.
In every face and attitude we see the pain and
consternation just produced by our Lord's speech.
"One of You shall betray Me." Judas the Traitor
seated rather apart on a low stool, scowls full
of terror, as about to escape out. The artist
has been credited with representing as Judas a
man then in high office in Freiburg who had
done him a wrong — but the same is told of
nearly every "Judas" extant — and let us believe that so highly gifted an artist as the sculptor Xavier Hauser was above the indulgence of
so petty a feeling in producing this his great
master-piece.

On the 16ᵗʰ August, 1805, the table spread in
front of our Lord was consecrated as an altar
by the Suffragan Bishop Graf Bissing — and
on Maunday-Thursday in the following year the
Blessed Sacrament was for the first time deposited
in the Ciborium held in our Lord's hand. —
On Maunday-Thursday, every year, Mass is now
celebrated at this altar. In 1878, by the liberality of a benefactress the figures were very aptly

and artistically coloured which adds greatly to the
life-likeness of the scene to which the devout
visitor of the Minster returns again and again
with reverent admiration. Most unfortunately —
for the better preservation of this admirable work,
a heavy grating of iron rods is soldered into the
wall in front of it, which precludes all possibi-
lity of any photograph of this work of art and
devotion, a loss keenly felt by all lovers of
Freiburg Minster and all collectors of interesting
souvenirs.

Nearly in front of this sacred spot rest the
bodies of the Archbishops as mentioned on page
65, and here the altar of St. Joseph stands out
across the north aisle — acting as a screen to
both the graves of the Archbishops — and to the
Abendmahlskapelle.

This altar was the work of Joseph Glaenz in
1828. The figures of St. Joseph, Abraham, David,
Peter, John and Andrew were from Munich.
Near the altar a stone marks the resting place
of Dr. Joseph Anton Schwartz, born 1743 — died
1818 — who, by his sound judgment, energy,
and liberality, greatly contributed to the restoration and preservation of the Minster.

3. Chapel of S. S. Peter and Paul.

At the north corner of the Romanesque transept
just where it joins the Gothic wall is a chapel

which once had beautiful windows and was embel-
lished with fine frescoes of which dim remains
can here and there be traced, of a Crucifixion
with St. Mary, St. John and St. Longinus &c. &c.

But long ago, the staircase, leading up to the
large gallery for the choir which fills the north
transept at a great height, was unavoidably placed
in this chapel, and it has become a sort of lumber-
corner ever since, being quite dismantled.

Passing an entrance door at the north end we
find ourselves facing the iron gates that screen
the beautifully restored chapel dedicated to

4. St. Anna and St. Alexander;

the recess under the music gallery being filled
with very old oaken seats and desks; and many
humble offerings in wax or other objects being
hung upon the spikes of the iron work of the
gate, as this corner is a most favourite resort
especially of the old and poor of the flock, and
is seldom without a few worshippers who pour
out their burthened hearts before the screen, or
at the foot of a life-sized figure of our Lord
bearing His cross — in painted wood — that
stands close beside the chapel archway, the base
of which, together with the ground He walks on,
are always buried beneath wreaths and bunches
of flowers, often brought from distant cottage
gardens and forest glens.

The painted windows of this chapel are beautiful specimens of that art at the commencement of the 16th century being placed by Johann Baldung in 1515 A. D. The Minster account books mention 12½ shillings paid to Master Johann Baldung by the guild companies for making the sketch for the painting of the St. Anna window. The paintings are now greatly faded, and the colours in many places have entirely vanished, leaving the windows of a greyish yellow and brown tint with good outlines and producing a most harmonious and artistic effect — far more so than they would if, (as has been done with some of the glass in the choir chapels) any attempt were now made to restore them to their pristine brilliancy. The windows represent the Holy Family surrounded by their kinsmen.

The Blessed Virgin sitting with the Saviour on her knee, is the central object — with the motto "Blessed Virgin Mother Mary, come to our help". Above, St. Joseph bears the motto: "Thy throne, O God, is for ever and ever." Near the Saviour, St. Anna to whom at first this chapel was dedicated, offers an apple to the Holy Babe, and St. Joachim bears a scroll with the motto "A flower shall blossom forth from his root".

Behind, a female figure, perhaps Elizabeth (?) with a motto, "A rod is sprung from the root

of Jesse". Above the figures of S. S. James and
John the Evangelist stands Salome their mother.
On the right hand is Mary the wife of Cleophas
reading a book, and beneath her are her children:
Judas, (or Jude) Thaddeus, Joseph, Justus, Simon
and James (the Lesser). Above is Cleophas himself
with the motto "He shall sit on the throne of
David for ever". The dedication inscription of
this window is as follows:

"This window is erected by the miners of the
"'St. Anna, Mine' to the praise of Almighty
"God, the Blessed Virgin and Saint Anna."

Up to the year 1650 this dedication remained.
But in that year a certain capucin Prior, one Dom
Raphael Schachtelin, was the Cathedral preacher
by appointment, and being called to the head
quarters of his Order, at the time of Pope In-
nocent X. on that occasion had permission to
take from the Catacombs the bones of St. Alexander, an officer of the martyred Theban Legion
who had been buried there after their massacre
in 302 A. D., which bones together with other
relics, he brought back and presented to the
twelve guilds of Freiburg. The chest containing
the relics had been officially sealed in Rome and
when opened at Freiburg they were attested by
the Rev. Sebastian Villinger, Chancellor, by Theo-
bald Bley, and by Heinrich Schmidlin, the Town
Clerk. On the 21ˢᵗ Sept. 1651, the relics were

solemnly and reverently carried to the St. Anna chapel, the abbot Roesch officiating.

The remains of St. Alexander are decorated by eight lbs. of pure gold, 40,000 pearls and 20,000 garnets. St. George, who had at first been Patron of Freiburg, was now formally re-elected and re-installed together with St. Alexander and St. Lambert, Patron of woolstaplers. In 1739 a new coin — a Thaler — was cast in honour of the new Patrons. Their names are inscribed together on a pillar of the Cathedral, and on a flag dated 1728 are the three Patrons depicted. Likewise as we have already seen, they are represented in the grand fresco of the east wall of the nave. St. Anna in fact has been dispossessed of her chapel and St. Alexander's memory is the present object of its existence. It has been recently re-decorated in excellent taste and with great elaboration, and the interpenetrating moulding, the distinctive mark of the architecture of Freiburg Minster as of most German Gothic, is seen to perfection at the intersections of the vaulted roof, the transomes and the walls. The altar and high reredos are admirably carved and worked in wood gilt and coloured, having a very rich and ancient effect — though probably comparatively modern.

5. Altar of the Magi or three Kings.

STANDING against the wall at the left side of the choir arch, is an altar with a very beautiful carving representing the Adoration of the Eastern Kings or "Wise Men". This altar was brought from a chapel of the old "Basler Domhof" in the Kaiser-Strasse of Freiburg, now No. 51, which building was occupied first by the Cathedral Chapter of Basle at the time of the Reformation at Basle. The altar was removed when the chapel containing it was cleared away for the sake of making space for the diligences when the Basler Domhof was made the principal post office. — The upper carving was by Josef Glaenz, in 1825, but has the appearance of far greater age. The figures on the shrine are by the artist Johann Wydynz, 1505 (whose name is carved beside them). They are noble and graceful but savour too much of the Renaissance style.

6. The Altar of S. S. Anna and Elizabeth.

ON the corresponding right hand side of the chancel stands this altar, also not originally in the Cathedral but replacing one dedicated to St. John of Nepomuk, which once stood here. The work of his altar was also done by Glaenz, but the sculptor of the interesting group over the altar is now unknown. St. Elizabeth, St. Anna and

the Blessed Virgin are playing with the Infant
Saviour, evidently teaching Him to walk, it is
most tenderly and reverently treated.

Innumerable side altars — some say 66 —
utterly without value and greatly detracting
from the dignity and simplicity of the Minster,
with which, since the year 1482 the walls had
gradually become encrusted, were swept away
in the Restoration. There were dedications to
S. S. S. Stephen, John, Nicholas, Peter and Paul,
St. George, St. Martin, St. Oswald, St. Sebastian,
St. Afra of Augsburg, St. Katharine &c. &c.

There are now but the four altars in the
nave of which the last we have to notice is by
far the most important viz: The altar of the
Blessed Virgin, or Frauenchörlein on the south
side close beside the chapel of the Entombment
already described.

The carving of this, also by Glaenz, was finished
in 1828. The figures of the B. V. M., of S. S.
Alexander, Lambert and others are much older.
The newer figures of apostles were the work
of Jacob Maier of Donaueschingen. This altar
is used for the reservation of the Blessed Sacrament, and is a great centre of church life. Vespers,
Litanies and Benediction, are given there most
evenings. Mass is celebrated there daily —
marriages performed &c. — and the altar steps
are hardly ever without kneeling worshippers.

The beautiful Memorial painting of our Blessed Lord close beside the altar steps, and the nearly effaced one of St. Martin on the wall above, have been mentioned among the frescoes. Close by is the tomb of A. Weber who died April 17. 1756, and who was a great benefactor to the Minster.

It now remains to us to inspect the choir and the adjacent chapels of the chevet, by which it is surrounded.

The Choir.

ASCENDING some stone steps we find ourselves close to a large and handsomely decorated but moveable altar, standing in the centre, at the top of the steps. From this altar the Blessed Sacrament is distributed to the communicants at our Lady's Mass daily.

To the right and left of this we observe at a moderate height above the ground, two heavy iron doors and gratings let into the solid stone wall of the towers that support the choir. These are the entrances to the recesses wherein are deposited all the archives of the Cathedral on one hand and of the town on the other. On the left wall are also two monuments set into the stone which were brought here from the Dominican monastery at the time of its dissolution in 1802

together with the remains of Count Conrad the II.
and his wife. The inscription in Latin says that
in the year 1350 on the 10th July died the Illu-
strious Count Conrad Lord of Freiburg and Land-
grave of Breisgau, and that on the last day of
Feb' 1331 died the Countess Anna of Freiburg
and Margravine of Breisgau.

Facing these on the right wall is the tomb of
General von Rodt, who died Feb' 17. 1743 after
54 years of faithful and gallant service to their
majesties the Emperors Leopold I, Joseph I and
Charles VI. of Austria, and the Empress Maria
Theresa. It is a good specimen of the sculpture
of that period, but looks singularly out of place
with its trophies and armour, cannon and balls,
in the precincts of the sanctuary. It was the
work of Christian Wenzinger, artist and magi-
strate, who died 1797.

Close beside the side entrances to the choir,
below the steps which rise to the high altar
are four recesses, in which stand four statues of
the Dukes of Zähringen, the work of Xavier
Hauser of Freiburg. — On the south side stands
the figure of Berchthold 3[d] in full armour, with
open vizor, with a plan of the Town of Freiburg
in his hand, and with this inscription: "Berchtold 3[d], son of Berchtold 2[d], Duke of Zähringen,
founder of this Town about the year 1118. He
held the reins of government from 1111 to 1123."

To the left is a statue of Berchtold 4ᵗʰ also in
armour with uncovered head, carrying a banner.
An inscription in old German sets forth that
Berchtold the 4ᵗʰ, a son of Duke Conrad of Zähringen, completed the Town and the Cathedral,
and died Sept. 1186. On the north side the
Duke Conrad kneels with uncovered head before
the Blessed Virgin, Patroness of the Minster. —
This Duke Conrad — brother to Berchtold the
3ᵈ — began the building of the Cathedral and the
Tower in 1123, and died before its completion
on the 31ᵗ May 1172.

Next stands the statue of Duke Rudolf,
Bishop of Liege, wearing his episcopal robes over
a suit of armour. —

An inscription tells us that Rudolf, son of
Conrad and brother of Berchtold 4ᵗʰ, as Bishop
of Liege brought to Freiburg the head of the
Blessed St. Lambert, and died August 1191.

In the year 1872 an inspection of the relics
took place, and there was found a portion only
of the head of St. Lambert. The top of the
scull was enclosed in a silver bust of the Bishop.
The relics of St. Lambert are now all enclosed
together in the large silver bust aforesaid. They
were formerly kept in the Lambert chapel of a
castle on the Schlossberg, now an utter ruin.
These relics were taken to the Minster in solemn
procession at Easter 1514.

On the silver base of the bust of the martyr
St. Lambert is inscribed in old German:

"Als man zalt M.C.C.C.C.LXVIII jar ist
"dis werch getr: (trieben) junker Hans
"Ulrich Meyer, Niclas Clewin von Bogsperg
"und Micheln Mittag der zyt uns . . . . lieben
"frowen pfleger und Hans heininger."

Tradition says that the Bishop Rudolf who took
part in the crusade under Frederic I, visited his
Zähringer kinsmen at their castle of Herdern, on
his way home, and that he died there, leaving
to his kinsmen the relics he had brought from
the Holy Land.

The Freiburg chronicles mention his death in
the year 1189 — but the year 1191 is on his
tomb as the date of his decease (or perhaps as
the date of his interment in the choir?).

On either side of the steps leading to the upper
end, or Priest's choir are two large candelabra,
resting on lions of brass, which were cast in
the year 1680.

A splendid corona for 24 tapers is suspended
from the centre of the choir and is of the same
date. To the left of the High altar stands the
throne of the Archbishops — placed there in
1848 and paid for from the Cathedral funds.

Considering that Gothic art was but then
emancipating itself from its long burial, much
credit is due to Glaenz, for his efforts, though it

is by no means a fitting Archiepiscopal throne, and is altogether too slender and meagre in design for its situation and its purpose, though a very elegant piece of workmanship. The figures of Temperance, Justice, Prudence and Strength were from Munich studios. On the right side of the altar is the Vesper choir of recent Gothic stone work.

Near this is hung against the wall the Sanctus bell, composed of a number of silver bells hung round a wheel, which as it is turned, gives out an exquisite clangour of musical sounds calling to the deep reverence of the "Ter Sanctus" or the still higher worship of "Him Who cometh in the name of the Lord". It is said that the Sanctus bell made in this fashion is an importation from Spain, and is even of Moorish origin.

The High Altar.

The choir and High altar as they now stand were solemnly consecrated on the 4th and 5th of December A. D. 1513, to the glory of God the Holy Trinity, to the B. V. Mary, the three Wise men of the East, the Holy Innocents and the Holy apostles, by order of the Bishop Hugo of Constance, by his Suffragan and Vicar-General Balthasar Bishop of Troy — a Dominican.

The great altar piece which is justly one of the glories of Freiburg, is a tryptich with seven subjects by Johannes Baldung Grien of Gmünd, and this, together with a picture by Holbein have been twice carried off by victorious French armies — once, on the 29. July 1797, and the second time in 1809, when, however, they went no further than Colmar, whence by the mediation of the G. Duke Charles Frederic they were both quickly returned to their places.

Baldung was of the Swabian school of art, and his style much ressembles that of Albert Dürer, under whom he had probably studied at Nürnberg, for among his papers and valuables was found a lock of Dürer's hair, cut off after his death. In the year 1496 Baldung painted a picture of the convent of Lichtenthal near Baden, of which his sister was then abbess.

The colossal wood work of the altar is by Josef Glaenz and Franz his son — done in 1831—33, the gilding and ornamentation by Josef Hauser. Above the altar stand three late Gothic figures carved in wood, of St. Conrad, Bishop, St. Stephen and St. Lawrence Deacons.

We will now turn our attention to the series of beautiful paintings on the tryptich, commencing with the centre which represents the Coronation of the B. V. M. — She kneels on floating clouds with flowing hair and folded hands —

her robe shines with gold, her mantle is of sea-blue.

The Almighty Father with crown and sceptre and royal robes sits to the left: God the Son with crown and terrestrial globe sits to the right, and both are holding a crown over the head of the B. V. Mary, while God the Holy Ghost hovers above all, in glory. In the upper part, proclaiming angels with trumpets surround the group — in the lower part children angels with wings but half grown, seem to sport round the Blessed mother, some peeping out from under her mantle like children at play. — In the corner a boy sings from a music book, and another plays a bass viol, or viola.

The whole is framed in a perfect master piece of wood-carving, in which angels and flowers are exquisitely blended.

On the two wings are figures of the apostles, on each side six. St. Peter and St. Paul being foremost, as witnesses of the solemn scene. — These are powerful and life-like figures. And when, as at Advent and Christmastide the side wings are closed, the following pictures are seen:

` *The Annunciation.* Mary kneels at a prayer desk placed in an open loggia, her book lies open before her, a vase filled with May-flowers is at her feet, and a light burns on a partly covered table.

A pure white mantle wrapped about her arms
falls down to the earth. Above her hovers the
Holy Ghost, the Infant Saviour seems to descend
from heaven bearing in His arms a Crucifix.
Mary has turned round to gaze upon the speaking
angel who, as God's representative, carries in his
hand a sceptre, and who points to the Child.
Mary's whole figure and attitude express the
utmost devotion and modesty.

The Salutation. In the midst of a beautiful
country scene "in the hill country of Judea"
is the Meeting of Mary and her cousin Elizabeth.
Mary is again clothed in white, with a mantle
of sea - blue, and a transparent veil covers her
golden hair; the innocence and charm of her
face are a striking contrast to the dignified
elderly figure of Elizabeth, who wears a robe of
crimson edged with fur and a thick white head
dress. At their feet play young hares, emblems
of fecundity.

The Nativity. A night scene. The eastern
star shines above the half ruined stable. In
the back is seen the closed gate of Bethlehem.
The whole light and brilliancy of the picture
emanates from the central figure, the Babe, who
stretches out His arms to Mary kneeling above
Him. St. Joseph leans forward from out the
darkness. In spite of much beauty this picture
is considered inferior in workmanship to the others.

The Flight into Egypt — the crown of the whole. The Holy Family is halting in the shade of a date-palm, Mary in a dark blue dress and graceful veil, with a sweet happy maternal aspect, is seated upon a mule gaily caparisoned. She holds a rein with her right hand, her left encircles her Child. St. Joseph is at the mule's head, with Rosary and staff in hand. On his shoulder a water bottle is slung. An unspeakably lovely group of angels gather dates for the Child, bending down the fruit-laden branches. One little angel has alighted on the mule's back, and steadies himself by holding a bough while he offers three dates to the Holy Babe. On the ground a goldfinch is pecking at a flower, plants of strawberry are in bloom and fruit on which snails creep and humble-bees rest. The date of this picture is 1519.

The Predella and its wood carving are also by Johann Baldung Grien. Right and left the corners are filled by shields bearing the Austrian and episcopal arms.

Back to back with Grien's great altar piece is another large picture of the Crucifixion, only seen from the ambulatory behind the choir. Christ is nailed on the cross between the two thieves. The left hand one writhes in despair while the right hand one confides in Christ. Mary sinks fainting into the arms of John, the weeping women sur-

round them while Mary Magdalene remains pros-
trate at the foot of the cross. Soldiers and spectators stand around, and a young man holds in one
hand a vase of vinegar and in the other the
reed and sponge. An old man gazing with gloom
upon the scene leans against the thief's cross
supporting himself on a lance. Behind him stands
the artist himself, a man of kindly face, wearing
a red cap, and a boy carries a tablet with the
arms of the artist. Beside this Crucifixion are
depicted St. George, St. Lawrence, St. John the
Baptist and St. Jerome with his lion. Underneath are portraits of some administrators of the
cathedral fund who stand in devout attention
before the picture of the Madonna of 1516 (19?).
The inscription is as follows:

"Sebastiano de Blumenegg, Patricio. Egidio
"Has, Udalrico Wirtner, Plebeis Magistrati-
"bus, Nicolas Shefer, edis sacre Thesaurariis,
"hoc opus factum. Ann. Sal. M. D. X. V. I."

To the left hand corner of the base we see
two lovely heads of angels, and in the right
corner is the artist's own memorial thus:

"Joannes Baldung cog. Grien Gamundanus
"Deo et Virtute auspicibus faciebat."

Passages under the Towers.

7. Entrances to the Ambulatory and Choir-Chapels.

THE choir is built against the two weather-cock
towers and on old foundations which were laid
in the year 1354. It is carried by 12 pointed
arches, through which the side chapels are seen —
and it is lit by windows above as well as those
of the side chapels. On either side of the choir
there are passages in the towers which lead from
the transepts to the ambulatory and the chapels
behind the High altar.

The passage to the north near the Alexander
chapel has nothing noteworthy — a number of
large common presses containing the banners,
papers, &c. &c. of some of the town guilds —
stand in this corner, out of the way.

But on the opposite side of the choir is an
arched doorway full of interest, the capitals
and carvings being worthy of deep attention as
some of the oldest stone work in the church,
carved with very ancient Christian allegories.

On the left or choirside of the doorway we
find a group of sea-nymphs, half woman, half
fish. One is seated and suckling a baby with
the same formation. On her shoulder is perched
a bird like a parrot. Before these stands up
a second woman or mermaid, whose hand is
upraised as if in warning.

May it be that these represent the monster-births, or powers of Preadamite nature, who prophetically feel that the advent of Man will introduce a new era? For next this group we find man in combat with a Wyvern or dragon, asserting his place as the Lord and Master of Creation. In the third group Man, having tamed the powers of nature, turns them alas! to account in combating his brother man — for we see two Centaurs, half-man, half gryphon, fighting each other with sword and shield — one shield being cleft by the sword of the adversary; scientific warfare is intended, with skilled method of attack and defence, not a mere outbreak of uncontrolled passion. Again these three groups may represent only the natural unrestrained evil impulses of mankind before the period when Civilization came to control and guide them, and in either case the three corresponding groups on the right hand of the doorway form a sequel to the story, for here, beginning with the centre group we see the Church, represented by a monk, who has so far secured the wild untamed Humanity, (represented as a huge animal) as to hold it tightly by a kind of *lasso* round its neck; but in spite of the tight hold, and hard blows of the monk the beast entirely refuses to submit to tuition, its whole will and energy are turned away from the dis-

cipline, and not only so, but it firmly holds its
offspring out of the way of education also.

To the left of this is Humanity, at last partially
subdued by the superior mental power, though
its whole attitude shows that the heart is still
untamed, the mind still rebellious; yet the beast
sits up facing the monk, though its head is still
averted, moreover it holds meekly enough a
book in one hand and a ferule in the other;
also the cudgel, no longer needed, rests on the
shoulder of the monk, while behind the beast
is seen his young one (the newer generation)
coming of its own will to the monk and beginning
the ascent of the "hill of difficulty" the road to
learning.

The last group to the right shows us the beast
perfectly tamed and trained, so that a woman
who sits astride upon it, turns its head towards
her and holds open its mouth. Does the woman
here typify the Church? or the fact that the
certain fruit of Civilization is the ascendancy of
woman's influence in the christianized world, as
her degradation is an inevitable mark of retro-
gression or of barbarism.

Another curious sculpture is seen in a corner
of the capital. A crowned man is seated in what
is evidently intended for a ship on the waves;
he holds a cross, or crozier in his hand, type
surely of the ark of the Church on the waves

of Time. To the mast and around the ship
strong ropes are attached, the ends of which are
tightly held on each side by a gryphon, representing either the endeavours of the powers of Evil
to sink the vessel and its freight — or perhaps
denoting that "overcoming of Evil by Good"
which compels even the powers of Evil to further
the cause of God's Church and speed her on her
way; "The fierceness of Man shalt Thou turn to
Thy praise". Ps. 76 v. 10.

In the middle ages Symbolism became a science,
and numerous treatises were written on the subject.
Symbols were taken from the Scriptures, from
Poetry and Fable, from Nature and even from
Mythology.

In these the powers of Evil, or the Devil
himself were symbolized by dragons, gryphons,
Wyverns or other huge beasts of fable. A peacock
was an emblem of immortality because its flesh
was supposed to be incorruptible — a parrot
was the type of Vanity &c. &c.

In the wall beyond these sculptures is a stone
on which is carved in relief the anointing of
David by Samuel, very roughly done, and supposed
to be the oldest carving in the Minster.

On the flat wall of the passage arch are deeply
incised memorials of two Cathedral Priests buried
probably in the crypt beneath, near the altars

they especially served. One of Karl Walk bears
the date of 1336, the other of E. H. von Geisingen
is dated 1827.

The Sacristy.

ON the door lintel of the sacristy is inscribed the
date 1480. A door leads into the south transept
close to the window lately filled with stained
glass by an English resident (before mentioned).
The fastenings of this door are of curious old
metal work. Above this door are figures of
St. Stephen and St. Katharine mingled with stone
work foliage. Over the door that opens towards
the choir are, on one side, the Annunciation, and
inside the Adoration of the Magi — in high relief.

There is in the sacristy a painting, left as
a legacy in 1809 by a Baroness von Pfirdt, which
is attributed to Luke Cranach or to Baldung
Grien. It represents the Resurrection of Christ,
with Mary and John. The size of the sacristy
is so limited that it would be insufficient even
for a Parish church, and for a large Minster it
is extremely inconvenient.

There are a few illuminated books, vestments
&c. &c. worth seeing; but the real valuables of
the Cathedral are not kept within its walls nor
is it easy to obtain an inspection of such as
there may be.

It has been whispered that some very precious jewel was once purloined by a visitor, and that, like King Hezekiah, the Authorities learned too late that it is best not to be too lavish in the display of treasures to passing strangers. But amongst these treasures ought to be mentioned the first spadeful of earth removed in placing the foundations of the Minster. It lies in a cylinder of glass and wrapped up in cloth of gold, the glass being mounted in silver of Byzantine work, and has thus lain for the best part of eight centuries.

The Spring or Well.

PASSING under the new organ and leaving the sacristy, we find ourselves close to the south choir-entrance from the market place — called the Door of Benediction from its proximity to the font, and here we come upon a running spring of crystal pure water, which falls from an opening in the wall into a large stone basin or pool hollowed to receive it. Over the fountain stands a pedestal bearing a large figure in coloured wood of the Blessed Virgin, on which is the date 1666, while on the reservoir that of 1673 is inscribed.

Those who delight to linger in the restful beauty and tinted shades of the dear old Minster,

or meditate awhile before the Abendmahlskapelle
or shrine of St. Alexander, when the church is
empty, and the voice of prayer and praise is
silent for awhile, well know how the unceasing
sound of that rippling water seems to become
the living voice of the solitary Minster itself,
raised in continual intercession, as generation
after generation of her children pass along, from
the font, washed by this pure stream, through
her aisles, on their road to paradise; and conveying to weary brain and tired limbs a sense
of peace and rest that words fail to express.

In the middle ages, wells were often placed
in churches in order that from a consecrated
and unsullied spring water should be obtained
for · all purposes of Divine Service, and these
were mostly protected by stone canopies to
which a pulley was attached for raising the water.

These are frequently placed in the sacristies
of Italian churches, as at the Certosa of Pavia,
at San Lorenzo at Florence, also at Ratisbon
and at Strasburg.

The fountain of Freiburg Minster, however,
comes rushing down from its sweet source among
the rocks and giant pines of the Black Forest,
and was led into the Minster in the year 1511.
Thence it goes out to join its many comrade
rivulets who keep the streets of Freiburg for
ever cool, clear, bright, and musical.

On the wall near the fountain are tablets to the memory of Reinwart Göldin, treasurer of the Cathedral of Basle 1660, and also of Georg Fladerer, Canon of Basle also buried here in 1610.

The Kapellen-Kranz, or Coronet of Chapels of the Choir.

8. Chapel of the Noble Family von Stürzel.

THIS chapel now serves as the baptistery of the Minster, and is half filled by a very large and heavy font of costly marble the work of Sebastian Wenzinger. The old font still remains in the nave near the altar of the B. V. M.

The altar is a specimen of the transition from Gothic to Renaissance, and was restored in 1867 by Sebastian Luz. The paintings are — a Bishop, St. Anthony of Egypt (the Thebaid), St. Roch, who devoted himself to care for the plague-stricken, and falling himself a prey to the disease, was miraculously cured by the touch of an angel. Inside the side wings are St. Christopher and St. Sebastian (in Patrician dress with the arrows of his martyrdom in his hand). In six divisions on the outer side are 42 Saints among which are the 14 Helpers of the Distressed namely: St. Vitus, St. Blasius, St. Cyriac, St. Pantaleon, St. George, ʻSt. Christopher, St. Eustace, St.

Katharine, St. Margaret, St. Barbara, St. Achatius, St. Aegidius, St. Dionysius and St. Erasmus.

The altar-piece represents the Descent from the cross. On the Predella God the Father supports the body of the Crucified; to the right is God the Holy Ghost, to the left hand the B. V. Mary, with her heart pierced with the sword of anguish.

There are some tombstones remaining here. One by the altar is to John Seb. Stürzel von BUOCHHEIMB — died 1661 — Between the escutcheons is written "Here I lie buried beneath the earth. What I am, must thou, reader, become also."

Another stone records the death, in 1714, of Johann Stephen Beyer of Buchholz, a noble.

The window represents the Adoration of the Magi, with St. Conrad of Constance (of the ancestral family of our Queen) and who was the Patron of the founder's family, which family is depicted as kneeling below. An inscription tells us that the portraits are Conrad Stürzel von Buochheimb and his lady Frau Ursula, date 1505.

This window has been admirably restored in 1876, in the atelier of Messrs. Helmle and Merzweiler, as has also that of

9. The University Chapel

which represents our Lord in the temple among the doctors of the Law; answering and asking

them questions, and which was placed in this
chapel in 1524.

The doctors are represented as searching the
scriptures and wondering at the Child's wisdom.
Mary and Joseph are just entering the door
overjoyed at finding Him after their three day's
loss. The remaining portions of the windows
contain the Patrons of the "Faculties": St. Luke
Evangelist, St. Katharine with the lily of innocence,
the laurel of knowledge, and the palm of martyrdom. St. John Evangelist and Hieronymus, or
Jerome, whose image is on the great seal of the
University. The altar piece of this chapel de-
serves our very especial notice as being the
work of John Holbein the younger, painted probably during his residence at Basle between
1529—1532 at the order of a Swiss family named
Oberried, as can be seen below the painting.

John Holbein, born at Augsburg in 1495 early
freed himself from medieval traditions, and followed the style of the German Renaissance and the
bent of his own genius. He was made a citizen
of Basle in 1520, but, finding the times were
not favourable in Germany, he removed to England with introductions from his friend Erasmus
to the celebrated Chancellor Sir Thomas More,
and met there with much success — finally end-
ing his days there in 1543. Basle, Copenhagen
and Berlin are rich in engravings by Holbein, and

he has left a very great number of paintings,
the palm being universally given to the celebrated Madonna belonging to the Burgomaster of
Basle, Meyer zum Hasen.

We have already seen that this altar-piece
was twice carried off by the victorious French
armies of 1796 and 1809, but it has had many
other vicissitudes. In 1596 the Emperor Rudolf II.
tried to get possession of it, but happily failed.
During the Thirty year's War it was carried to
the Palace of the Bishop of Constance at Schaff-
hausen. Thence it wandered to Munich at the
petition of the Elector Maximilian, who wished
to see it. — In 1652 it went to the Emperor
Ferdinand 3ᵈ, at Regensburg, who was greatly
interested about it. It then remained in peace,
till the French invasion before named, 1796 —
when it was taken, together with the great fold-
ing High altar piece, to Paris — and again
in 1809, but this time as far only as the neighbouring town of Colmar.

The subject of this so highly esteemed and
coveted picture is on two tablets — the Nativity
on one, the Adoration of the Magi on the other.

In the first the Holy Babe is laid on some
straw wrapped in swaddling clothes, the brilliant light emanating from Him lights the whole
scene — the young mother, kneeling in devout
contemplation, St. Joseph with the wondering

6*

shepherds, the adoring attendant Angels, the shepherd's faithful dog which lies near the Babe, and an ox, whose head is alone visible. The lower portion of the picture is thus flooded with His glory while the upper portion is lit by the moonlight which shines full through the ruined roof of the hall.

The second picture represents the same or a similar building — a hall, also with a ruined and broken roof; across the aperture a swallow is flitting, and the guiding star also shines in the dawning light of morning. A group of variously clothed attendants with camels, horses &c. are very dimly seen in the back as well as some other spectators seen pointing up to the star they had followed, but the interest of the picture is concentrated upon Mary, the Babe upon her knee, the old king who kneels before Him in a robe of brilliant red bordered with ermine, the second king, who offers myrrh — and, most especially, upon the Moorish king, clothed in a flowing white robe embroidered and edged with gold, in whose hands is the vase from which rises the fragrant cloud of the frankincense — these form a group matchless in composition and in brilliancy of colour, and in exquisite detail.

The altar itself came first from Basle Cathedral to the University of Freiburg, and as it was consecrated in 1554 it was probably then first

placed where it stands. It was beautifully repainted and restored in 1866 by Sebastian Luz,
partly at the expence of the University. On the
Predella of the altar is inscribed:

An. Dom. MDLIIII die XVII octo. altare hoc
consecratum est in Dei honorem et beatae Mariae
Virginis S. Joannis Evang. St. Hieronymi, divi
Ivonis, St. Lucae Evang. Beatae Katharinae
Virg. et mart.; a R. D. Suffrag. Constantiense
D. Jacobo Elmer impositis de more reliquiis cer-
tis D. Laurentii, St. Nicolai, et SS. decem mil-
lium martyrum, the latter being bones of some
of the Theban Legion from St. Maurice.

The altar wings are not by Holbein, and have
on them good paintings of the Four Doctors of
the Church: Augustine of Hippo, St. Jerome, St.
Gregory and St. Ambrose.

Near the altar is a wooden tablet with a
portrait of Michael Küblin of Kisslegg, who made
a foundation to the University and was, in many
ways, a great benefactor to the Minster.

The University chapel, and the large space in
the ambulatory in front of it, has been much
used as the burial place of learned professors to
whom there are many memorial tablets and stones.

10. Chapel of the Nobles of Lichtenfels and Krozingen.

In the window of this chapel (also restored
by Helmle in 1876) we see, in the first division,

the founder Cornelius von Lichtenfels, Canon of Basle, kneeling at the feet of St. Germanus. In the second division, Hans von Lichtenfels and his wives kneel before a picture of our Saviour. In the third, Christoph von Krozingen, A. D. 1524, before St. Christopher, and in the fourth, Truprecht von Krozingen and his two wives kneel before St. James the Greater. Over the altar is a picture of the Annunciation inferior perhaps as to execution but yet sufficiently attractive, an offering presented by William Blarer — a Canon of Basle. This altar was consecrated in 1615, but the ironwork of the gate bears the date of 1538.

On the wall is a memorial tablet with a Descent from the Cross and the inscription "A. D. 1617 1. Oct. died in this Vale of Misery the Noble Reinhard von Dettingen, last of his race and name. May the good God grant everlasting bliss to his and to all Christian souls. Amen."

This chapel has from this been also called the Dettingen Chapel. On the floor are two stones dated 1525 and 1563 respectively — the first marks the resting place of Cornelius von Lichtenfels, Canon of Basle and Provost of Grossthal abbey — the second of Christoph von Krozingen Chaplain of the Minster.

11. Chapel of St. John the Baptist, or of the Nobles of Snewlin.

THE windows again are restored by Helmle. Divison 1. The founder von Snewlin kneels before a St. John with the lamb. Div. 2. St. John is beheaded before a tower. Div. 3. Herod and Herodias at table, their eyes turned towards the daughter who, accompanied by other maidens brings in the head of St. John in a huge dish.

The dedication and memorial written beneath run thus:

"The noble knight Johan Snewlin — surnamed Greszer — has taken care that this work should be commenced in piety, and after his death his heirs have happily concluded it."

A new Gothic altar is a work of art executed, in 1869, by X. Marmon of Sigmaringen. In the centre is a Descent from the Cross of much beauty — over the tabernacle is St. John the Patron of the chapel — to left and right the aged Simeon and the Prophetess Anna. The former being the prophet of Mary's grief, and the latter his witness to that prophecy.

On the Predella two angels hold the "true image" of our Lord impressed on Veronica's kerchief. On the antependium are half length figures of David, Solomon, Isaiah and Jeremiah with texts of their prophecies of our Lord's sufferings. The carved ornamentations are angels with instruments of Christ's Passion. There stood formerly in this chapel a high altar presented by the family von Snewlin, a member of which was often elected Burgomaster. Over it was a painting of the Blessed virgin receiving the dead Saviour from the Cross, usually called "a Pieta". The paintings and carvings have been distributed between the two adjacent chapels.

There is on the wall a painting of the raising of Lazarus with a curious and interesting inscription-date of 1560, recording the virtues of the Suffragan Bishop, Mark of Lydda, i. p. i., formerly Dean of Basle and later a Professor of Freiburg University, who attained to great piety, learning, and all academic honours, and who required nothing of this world's good for himself beyond a burial place in this chapel opposite the altar, so that the Priest in celebrating the holy Eucharist might ever remember him.

On the wall is also a plate of gilded copper placed in 1702 commemorating John Sigismund Stapf for 52 years a teacher at the University, of which he was 22 times elected Rector. Johann Weidenkelter, Canon of Basle, is buried in front of this chapel — date 1653.

12. The first Kaiser Chapel.

THIS and the adjoining chapel were founded by the Imperial family of Austria, their arms are seen on the windows and on the keystone of the arch. The coloured glass represents on one side the Emp. Charles 5ᵗʰ at a Prayer desk before St. James of Compostella, Patron of Spain — with the date 1528. And on the other side is King Ferdinand kneeling before St. Leopold. The Inscriptions are as follows :

"Carolus D. F. Cle. Rom. Imp. semper Aug. Hispaniarum, Sicilie Rex, Archidux Austrie, Dux Burgundie, Comes Tyrolis."   .

"Ferdinandus D. G. Hungarie et Bohemie Rex, Infans Hispaniarum, Archidux Austrie, Dux Burgundie, Comes Tyrolis."

A new Gothic altar painted and gilt, the work of X. Marmon of Sigmaringen was placed . here on the Feast of the Immaculate Conception 8. Dec. 1875. The centre represents the Blessed virgin surrounded with angels before God the Father and God the Holy Ghost. Joachim and Anna her parents are near her. Scenes from her life are sculptured in small, and on either side are St. Bernard of Clairvaux and St. Bernard of Baden; under them a half length figure of Pope Pio IX. and the Archbishop Hermann of Vicari. The painted antependium has: The Fall of man, the Promise of the Saviour, the expulsion from Paradise, the Burning Bush, Aaron's budding rod, and the Vision of St. John in Patmos.

In this chapel is a monument to Canon Georg Hänlin, once Priest of this Cathedral, died 1621.

13. The second Kaiser Chapel.

On these windows are St. George and St. Andrew, Maximilian and Philip of Spain.

The altar was restored and arranged by Glaenz from part of the Snewlin high altar. The Baptism of Christ and the Vision at Patmos are painted with extreme minuteness in every detail. Till the year 1606 this chapel had no endowment. But at that date Dr Christopher Pistorius presented it with funds which provide for divine services therein. He held very high appointments as Apostolic "Proto-notar", member of the chapel at Basle, Provost of the collegiate Chapter of St. Martin at Colmar, and member of the Austrian Council, Doctor of Theology and Priest of this Cathedral. He died in 1628.

The picture represents the dead man restored to life by being thrown into the grave of the prophet Elisha. Kings' IV. Ch. 13, v. 21. A tablet representing the Coronation of the Virgin and surrounded by numerous small coats of arms, is

the memorial of a Dean of Basle Nicholas von
Brinikoffen, who was buried here 1576. The
iron gate bears the date of 1572.

We now stand behind the high altar of the
choir, and can see the picture of the Crucifixion
before mentioned — by J. Baldung Grien — and
in the centre of the space behind the high altar
we find a large and elegant stone fountain of
two basins with 11 jets for water made by Theod.
Kaufmann in 1511.

This fountain is supplied with water, but only
plays twice in every year, namely on Corpus
Christi and on the festival of the Patrons of the
town, September 17.

14. Chapel of the Cathedral Provost von Boecklin.

THE left hand window has an interesting subject,
namely the pilgrimage of the founder and his
wife to Spain. They are seen before a church
which is entered by a high flight of steps, and
is undoubtedly that of St. James of Compostella.
St. James stands crowning the two pilgrims, who
have shown their devotion by this long journey
to his shrine to ask his intercession on their
behalf. The right hand window shows St. Ursula
on a ship full of her companions, opposite Cologne,
where the Huns received them with a flight of
arrows, and caused their martyrdom.

Over the altar with a Renaissance bordering, is a large Byzantine silver Crucifix brought over at the time of the Crusades and given by Provost Boecklin. On it Christ is represented as the willing sacrifice without any expression of pain or suffering — the feet on a rest — the symbols of the four Evangelists on the four arms of the cross. A lamb is placed at the head and feet of the Christ. The cross is said to contain a small portion of the veil of the B. V. M. The tombs of the Boecklin family, who richly endowed the chapel, are here.

15. The Sother's, or St. Francis' de Sales Chapel.

THE three founders of this chapel are seen on the left division of the window with St. Paul. On the right are St. Peter and the Virgin and Child. Above the founders are texts appropriate to the apostles and B. V. M.; for St. Paul — "Tu es vas electionis", for St. Peter — "Tu es pastor ovium"; for St. Mary — "Sub tuum praesidium confugimus". An old inscription commemorates the founders thus: "An. MDXXIII factum est hoc sacellum impensis Joannis Petri et Pauli Sotherum fratrum", and a new one of 1876 states that the Marbe family caused these windows to be fully restored by Helmle and Merzweiler. Over the altar is a painting on canvass of St. Francis de Sales. Some tombs of no note are in this chapel.

16. The Locherer-, or St. Martin's Chapel.

THIS window has on it the Temptations of St.
Anthony. St. Benedict on whom Christ is smiling
from his cross, St. John Evangelist at Patmos,
and St. Martin and the beggar.

Nicholas Locherer Dean of Freiburg and John
Locherer, both masters of arts, founded and endowed
this chapel in 1520. The reredos is an excellent
carving of the 15ᵗʰ century, the centre piece representing the Virgin and Child, her mantle being
spread out to protect a row of figures of persons
of all ranks — from Pope and Emperor downwards.
The figures are admirably individualized, and it
is a most interesting and masterly production.
On each side of the centre, which has been robbed of its side-wings, are figures of St. Benedict and
St. Anthony of Egypt, and above stand St. John
Evangelist, St. Martin, and St. Sebastian. Before
the altar is the tomb of Jacobus Streit, who was
councillor for 40 years under Maximilian II.,
Rudolf II. and the Archduke Ferdinand, and
who died in 1640.

Between this chapel and the next is the north
choir-gate, the foundation-stone of which was
laid in 1354 on the Vigil of the Annunciation,
therefore the B. V. M. and the angel Gabriel
are represented in the keystone of the arch.

On the pediments are scenes from the Passion.
The soldiers casting lots on the Lord's vesture &c.

17. Chapel of the Nobles of Blumenegg, or St. Mary Magdalen's chapel.

ON the window is Christ appearing to St. Mary
Magdalene — and Christ on the Mount of Olives
with his Disciples — also two members of the
Blumenegg family. The inscription is half effaced.
The Annunciation, forming the altar piece, was
brought from the Snewlin chapel. Many of the
Blumenegg family are here interred.

18. The Chapel of the Nobles of Pennehofer

is an empty chapel. The windows are made
up of pieces and figures from other windows.
We trace the Descent from the Cross, and beneath
this kneel the founder and his wife, but the
inscriptions are imperfect. In this, as in all the
Kapellen-Kranz and ambulatory, an immense number of the noble families of Freiburg have for
many generations been buried.

The Choir-Organ.

ABOVE the choir in a gallery - recess to the
right, and partly built in above the sacristy
passage, was placed in 1882 a splendid new or-

gan from the well known factory of Herrn Wal-
ker in Ludwigsburg, Wurtemberg. This is the
one now in general use, and the nave-organ is
heard only on festivals.

Architecture and Measurement.

THE last restoration of the Minster was under-
taken in the year 1866 by the very Rev. Canon
Marmon who then held the office of Dompfarrer,
and completed by Herrn Domcapitular Rudolf
Behrle, who succeeded to the post of Dompfarrer in 1873, with the assistance of the Charity
commissioners. Their first act was to purify the
beautiful red sandstone interior from the coat
of vile grey wash that had defaced it for many
years. Under this they were fortunate enough
to discover some fairly well preserved traces of
old painting and gilding, which sufficed to form
a good plan for redecoration, convinced as they
were that their faithful reproduction would certainly prevent many blunders, and be also a tri-
bute due to the piety of their ancestors. It is
strange to say that the decorations of the
year 1547 were scarcely recognizable, while those
of the 14th century were in good condition, and
were entirely repainted by Wilhelm Weber, and
gilt by Josef Reichenstein of Freiburg. The
painting of the vaulted roofs with stars, flowers

7*

and plants, is an ornament, but also a symbol, giving, as in other places already mentioned, artistic expression to the picture language of the Scriptures, see Daniel 12 ch. 3 v. "They that turn many to righteousness shall shine as stars for ever." In Ps. 92 (English version). "The righteous shall flourish like a palm tree and spread abroad like a cedar." In Isaiah 35 ch. "They (the righteous) shall flourish like lilies" &c. &c.

Since this restoration was completed, the Interior of the Minster presents an imposing sight. The nave is carried by twelve mighty piers which are so constructed that between the four chief half columns there are three smaller ones with deep channels between them, the whole forming a clustered column.

On the nave side, the larger half-column with four smaller ones rises up without interruption to about the middle of the upper windows where the capitals receive the ribs of the vaulted roof. The half columns to the right and left carry on their capitals the nave-arcade, and those behind support the aisle vault. The piers have the Attic base with foliage or animals' heads at the angles of an octagonal plinth. The cup-shaped capitals of the columns are decorated with varied foliage. — A gallery runs the whole length of the nave under the clerestory windows, carried on a beautiful line of columns with excellent ca-

pitals, similar to those in Strasburg Cathedral.
The carved stone balustrade of this gallery as
well as that of the open chapel at the end of
the nave, dates from the end of the last century.

The vault of the nave is a quadripartite vault,
each bay being divided into four triangular spaces by the crossing ribs. With the exception of
the centre wide opening most of the bosses are
excellently carved and represent heads, among
them a Bacchus and a Devil! The earlier bosses are of the Romanesque type. — The Transepts are late Romanesque and have quadripartite vaults. In the centre is a cupola, the exterior
of which is now hidden by the roof. The lower
part is built in free stone with a beautiful den-
til cornice, and higher up it becomes circular.

To bring the square into the octagon, four
pendentives are inserted to obtain a support for
light groins. To enliven the appearance of the
western wall, a false triforium has been built.

At the north and south ends of the transept
are erected two galleries, or "loggie" in the very
finest Renaissance style, which once formed a
Lectorium dividing the choir from the nave, built
in the 16th century by one Jacob Altermadt.
It was evidently intended as a raised stage for
musicians and singers and consisted of three
arches, the centre one being filled by an altar,
the others with gratings. In the year 1789 this

lectorium was removed at the suggestion of Dr. Schwartz the precentor, and was erected in its present position where its serves as a screen to both the north and south entrance doors, and is thus made extremely useful — but, beautiful as these two screens are in themselves, they form a most unharmonious features in the transepts.

In old days the floor of the nave had come to be entirely paved with grave stones, doubtless many of them would now have been full of historical interest, but at the time of the great Restoration 1818—19 so often referred to, under Dr. Schwartz and his committee, the floor was entirely renewed and paved with tiles.

According to the builder's plan the breadth of the nave between the centres of the piers is 11.41 metres.

That of the south aisle is 9.3 metres.

That of the north aisle 9.25 metres.

The entire length of the building is 124.8 metres, that is, from the chapel wall to the High altar 10.2 metres, from the High altar to the steps of the transepts 42 metres, from the steps to the great west door 52.8 metres. Thence to the outer edge of the porch 19.8 metres. The nave is 27 metres high and the cupola 30 metres high. In Otte's Handbook of Archaeology the dimensions are given thus in Rhenish feet. The entire superficies (after subtracting that of

the piers, and all spaces not intended for worship) is 30,101 square feet = 2948.96 square
metres — the breadth of the nave is 32 feet
and the height 85 feet. The noticeable architectural irregularities in the interior of the Cathedral are worthy of remark. Were they originally designed for constructional, symbolical
or other reasons? Are they to be attributed to
want of care and accuracy? It is difficult to
decide. But at the time when the grey wash
was scraped from the interior, it was found that
the scaffolding used at the east end of the nave
was too short to reach quite across the west
end, and on the other hand the easterly columns
are 0.43 inches further apart then the westerly
ones. The aisle vault is said to follow the rise
of the Minsterplatz, on which the Minster stands
rising from west to east, but it is of course
imperceptible. We have also seen that the north
aisle is narrower than the south.

If the spectator stands in the exact centre of
the doorway, under the pedestal of the beautiful
Madonna, and looks at the centre point of the
choir, he will find that the apsis of the nave bends
noticeably to the south. Probably it is due to
this bend that the nave narrows towards the east.
Many Gothic churches in old days were purpo-
sely thus built. Notably so the beautiful old
Cathedral of Coire or Chur date 800 A. D. The

poetic piety of the ages of faith originated the
beautiful idea of the Cruciform building for
churches — a form, not representing the *cross*,
but the body of the crucified — *cruciformed* or
conformed to the crucified.

The altar is bent towards the south typical
of the sacred head of Christ as it falls in death
towards his heart. His right arm is nailed towards
the north — region in old times of the heathen and
of evil spirits, see Zephaniah Ch. 2 v. 13. His
left arm stretches to the south to gather His
bride to His heart. These are the north and south
transepts. In places where the men are seated
on the north side, it is that their strength is
that of the Lord's right hand, while the women
seated to the south are tender with the love of
His heart. If the men sit on the south side, it
denotes that their strength is perfected by the
tenderness of Christ, while the women on the
north side are made strong out of weakness by
the power of His right hand.

So the body of the Church is the "nave", ship
in which like the Deluge-ark men are saved:
while the Chancel, or choir as in old ships, is
highly raised for those whose duty it is to work
the ship. St. Paulinus of Nola writes (A. D.
410) "Twofold the roof, like the testaments
twofold, the nave loftier outside, but within de-
stitute of any symbol of God's special presence

corresponding to the old testament with its
temporal blessings and promises; while the new
with its temporal humiliation and its spiritual
glory is like the chancel, meaner and lower outside but *all glorious within*".*)

The Interior of the Tower.

AND now, before leaving the Minster, let us ascend the tower by the winding stone stairs which,
by pushing open a door we find on the south
side of the great west entrance-door, sixty five
steps will bring us to the great gallery (already
spoken of) over the west door, with a carved stone
balustrade and open to the nave of the Minster.
This is known as the St. Michael chapel and its
whole breadth is open to the nave of the Church
through a high arch. It forms the first story of
the tower. It was an old custom to build chapels
dedicated to the angels, on mountain heights and
in Gothic towers, and St. Michael the archangel
is the protector of the German flag.

An altar stands by the wall where Mass has
been occasionally celebrated, and in the centre
of the pavement is a large round well with parapet, which is repeated on each floor of the
tower. By this the tower-keepers have their

---

*) From "The Meaning of Christian Ritual" by the
Rev. H. H. Jeaffreson.

chief communication with the world below, and through it their food is sent up, as they are allowed no fire at any time — and every thing must go up ready cooked. Above this chapel the west wall is occupied by a grand west window restored in 1875 by Helmle and Merzweiler. — In the centre is the coat of arms of the Grand Duchy of Baden with the date 1805, when Freiburg was given over by Austria, to whom it had before belonged (with a short interval) since the year 1368. Beneath the Baden arms to the left, is the so-called Zähringen coat of arms with the lion, and the date 1120. — The Zähringen shield (which has no lion, only an eagle) to the right is the coat of arms of the Counts of Freiburg, with the date 1219.

In the centre are the arms of the Minster — a cross, the lower beam of which is split up. Beneath it again, we see the municipal arms — a cross with a raven's head.

Just before entering the door of the St. Michael we come upon a little dwelling, built among crockets, finials, gurgoyles and sculptured galleries, surrounded by an army of giant martyrs and saints, and commanding a charming view of the market place and the oity roofs and towers. In this little abode is found an old care-taker — whose husband, two stories higher up, looks out for fires. In exchange for 20 pfennigs she will

give you a pass which is to be delivered to the
guardian on the next floor. And now, passing
through the St. Michael chapel, we ascend a north-
west turret stair by 150 steps, to the dwelling of
the tower keepers who watch over the town and
Minster day and night, and who keep themselves
warm by dint of furs and flannels, in this exposed
and solitary situation. This floor is exactly like
the inside of some old ship, supported by immense beams, with unexpected little recesses and
windows at all angles and heights, making
it by no means a dreary or comfortless dwelling,
but quite the reverse; and, besides, in this room
they have the cheerful presence of the great
clock and the care of its wonderful and beautiful machinery, constructed at Strasburg by
Schwilgué, and placed here in the year 1851.

Striking clocks with wheels and weights were
first mentioned in 1120, but do not appear to
have become common in public buildings till the
middle of the 14ᵗʰ century. Strasburg had one
in 1352, and Augsburg in 1364. These were
the first large clocks known in Germany. The
old clock for many years in Freiburg tower, besides striking the hours and the quarters, showed
the changes of the moon.

The Bells.

FROM the side of the tower-keeper's apartment a rough wooden staircase leads up to the bells.

The frame work which occupies several stories is at least 60 feet high, and is constructed of gigantic beams fixed together by wooden bolts. As these bolts are driven into the walls and the space between the beams and the walls is so narrow that they could not have been inserted after the walls were completed, it is evident that the bell-stage must have been erected first. The existing ring of bells consists of three old, and ten new ones, as follows:

1. The Hosanna (popularly and familiarly called by Freiburgers "Susanna") weighing 100 cwt. and its tongue 400 lbs — has this inscription: Anno Domini MCCLVIII. XV Klas. Augusti structa est campana. O rex gloriae, veni cum pace. Me resonante pia populo succurre Maria. i. e.: "In the year 1258 on the 18th of July this bell was cast. O King of glory bring peace! When I sound, come to the help of the people, Holy Mary!" The note is E Flat.

2. The eight o'clock bell (called the Silver bell). Note F, weight 65 lbs., has no inscription. Its name is said to denote a good mixture of silver in its composition.

3. The Vesper bell weighing 80 lbs., cast in the year 1606 by Hans Ulrich Buitzlén in Breisach, bears, besides the names of the maker, the inscription: Venite exultemus Domino, jubilemus Deo salutari nostro. "Come let us praise the Lord and rejoice in God our Saviour." Note B.

In the year 1842 the following additional bells were cast by Karl Rosenlächer in Constanz at the expence of the Cathedral trust fund and cost 15,793 Gulden.

4. Christus (Logos) weight, 6852 lbs. Note B flat.

5. Maria, 3158 lbs. Note D.

6. Petrus 1772 lbs. Note F.

7. Paulus, 1576 lbs. Note F sharp.

8. Johannes 891 lbs. Note A.

9. Jacobus 711 lbs. Note B flat.

10. Alexander and Lambertus, 517 lbs. Note C sharp.

11. Schutzengel, (guardian angel) 362 lbs. Note D.

In the year 1843 two benefactors ordered from the same maker two more bells.

12. Konrad, 204 lbs. Note F.

13. Michael, 86 lbs. Note B flat.

This last bell was recast in the year 1866 by the brothers Koch, because it was cracked.

The ringing of the Bells.

SINGLE bells are rung as follows:

Maria. Daily at the midday "Angelus". "The angel of the Lord appeared unto her and said "Hail &c."

Hosanna. Every Friday at 11 o'clock, memorial of the crucifixion. — The "tenebrae &c." Every Thursday evening, memorial of the Agony in the Garden of Olives. — Every Saturday evening, memorial of all departed Souls. —

Petrus. Every evening at 9 oclock a "curfew warning people to be careful of fire and lights called "St. Agatha Chime".

Paulus. For morning and evening prayer, or Angelus.

In the year 1330 the Pope John XXII introduced the use of the triple Angelus throughout Christendom as a memorial of the Incarnation of Christ.

Jacobus is a sign of death and funerals.

Alexander and Lambertus rings for "Salve" and Vigils.

The Silver bell rings daily for early Mass, and at 8 o'clock every evening for a quarter of an hour.

———

We must here mention several old bells which unfortunately have been melted down. There were seven of them. — *A Sermon bell,* with the inscription: "A. D. MCCLXXXI. VIII Kal. Apr.

Ave Maria gra. O rex gloriae. Rex Xpe. Veni cum Pace."

The Prayer bell with the inscription: "A. D. MCCC. O Rex gloriae. Rex Xpe Veni cum Pace."

The Passing bell with the Sickingen coat of arms and the inscription: "Hans Friederich Weitnauer cast me. I flowed out of the fire at Basle in 1735. The daily "Salve" bell, without inscription which rang for the Salve Regina Meditation, a custom introduced in the year 1481 by Ulrich Spir."

The Tax bell which from Martinmass to Xmas rang twice a week for the collection of the town dues. On it was a string of names of various town worthies.

The Vigil or brother-hood bell. Inscribed: "Blessed are they who hear the word of the Lord and keep it." MDLXX.

The Hour bell which was hung on a scaffold above the others.

Leaving the keeper's room we again mount 54 steps and emerge on a broad leaded gallery surrounding the whole tower, commanding interesting views all over the roof and its adorning sculptures and statues — over the town and the spreading plains beyond — and over the nearest Black Forest hills.

The Spire.

AND now the visitor who possesses a good
courage and a fairly steady head must follow a
stair which winds round the outside of a turret
among the fine pillars and open work which as-
sisted by a few iron bars, forms in fact a thorough-
ly efficient protection, and through which not
even the most blundering of persons could fall
by any accident. 70 steps land the visitor on
the great stone platform which forms the roof
of the tower and the base of the huge pyramid,
of what might be the consolidated point-lace of
a world of giants. Nothing ever seen in carved
stone-work can surpass the beauty of this spire,
its exquisite Gothic tracery, its almost cobweb-
like appearance, as one lies back and looks up
the inside of this pyramid seen against the back
ground of a sky of sapphire blue here, so far
above the pigmy town at its foot, where for
600 of years the great stone angels have kept
guard round the dainty fragile handiwork of
generations long since turned to dust. And well
could one fancy that living angels might pause
on this spot in their flight on some errand of
mercy so pure, so still, so consecrated does it
seem; while the beautiful world stretches out
north, south, east and west till sky and earth
melt together in the regions far away.

To the west rises the noble and historic Kaiserstuhl, and far beyond the silver Rhine, stretches the line of the Vosges — "the blue Alsa-
tion mountains" with outline so varied and colouring so soft.

To the south near the outskirts ot the town
are the Schneeberg, the chapel and beech crowned
point of the Loretto - Berg, the bright glades
of Güntersthal, and the wooded Bromberg — close
beside the spire rise the Schlossberg and the
Rosskopf, with their forest crowned gardens —
while, to the north, the long spurs of the Black
Forest mountains embrace and protect the far
stretching flat plains of the March as far as Riegel,
generally of the strangest and loveliest tint of
grey green, and with many bright spots of clear
still water, or rushing streams. Last point of
all, against the sky the spire is completed by a
Fleur de lys in stone, 2 metres 10 c. high (its
pretty German name is Kreuzblume), and to
the apex of this is attached a star of gilded
metal forming a weather cock, and moveable by
the winds, giving due notice of change and storm,
and ever recalling to mind that star which "came
and stood over where the Child Jesus was"
dwelling, fitting termination to this fair casket
where all man has of his best, has for generations been lavished, to form not too unworthy a
dwelling place for His glorious presence. On

the stone floor under the spire is deeply engraved
the figure of one of the old stars, still preserved in
the town collection of Antiquities, to give an idea
of its great size, (1 m. 02 c.) though from its elevation it looks from the market place beneath, but
little larger than the real stars in the vault of
the heavens above it.

The star has occasionally to be trimmed, or
set in order, and the stone lace work has also
to be closely inspected. On the birthday of the
Grand Duke, Sept. 9th, three of the Minster work-
men perform the terrific feat of climbing up the
outside of the spire, clambering from one gigantic thread to another as a spider traverses his
web, till the star is reached, and every join of
the stone work has been examined and made
good, after which they fire off pistols to give
notice that their work is done, and that they
may claim a reward from the Archbishop. From
the top of the Fleur de lys to the earth the
measure is 115,845 m. (Baden measure 386'5".
English measure 330 feet $1^3/_8$ inches.)

———

It only remains to us to notice on leaving
the Minster by the western porch, three tall
pillars on handsome bases, which stand facing
the entrance. On the centre one is the Blessed
Virgin, and on the others stand St. Lambert and

St. Alexander, Patrons of Freiburg. These are
of no antiquity and have no historical interest
whatever, but they greatly enhance the pictu-
resqueness of the scene, and complete the unique
individuality of the Minster and its surroundings.

L'Envoi.

O peerless Minster! thou
Fit emblem of the body of thy Lord!
Whose sculptured stones and storied windows
Preach sermons thrilling the attentive heart.
Me seems thou art more meet for heaven, than earth.
But, though thy walls must pay the debt of sin and
         perish,
God grant *such* and *so many* Saints be reared in thee,
That in the heavenly country thou again may'st live
A lovely Spirit-Minster, yet more fair to see,
A joy of jewels to the Sacred Heart.

A. HOLIDAY.

Finis.

Addendum to page 79.

Chapel of the Entombment.

UPON the South side of the Nave, and close to the Altar where the Blessed Sacrament is reserved, is a remarkable Easter sepulchre, still in use. This sepulchre was added to the existing church in the year 1578. In the breast of the recumbent figure of our Lord is a small cavity (closed by lock and key) in which the Holy Sacrament is deposited with great ceremony, upon Good Friday, whence, on the Eve of Easter Day, It is removed (at 6 P. M.) during a very beautiful Service, known as "1 be Resurrection", (the first Easter Service) to the High Altar.

In front of the Sepulchre is a representation of the watching Roman Soldiers, overcome by sleep. The exquisite painted glass was painted by the brothers Helmle, of Freiburg, in the year 1825, the subjects being a continuation of those upon the opposite side of the building, from designs by Holbein.

Visitors to Freiburg at Eastertide should, on no account omit to be present in the Cathedral at the "Service of the Resurrection".